THE BALLAD OF THE BORAG - 1

A TALE OF LEVANTHRIA

A.P BESWICK

A.P BESWICK
PUBLICATIONS

Acknowledgments

This book is different from what you are used to in the series as it is a cozy fantasy. So I would like to dedicate it to you. Sit back in your comfy pyjamas, put your feet up and have your chosen drink at hand.

Most of all enjoy.

Acknowledgments

This book is dedicated to my beloved grandma Helena
Powell who passed away at the age of 95 in January.
It is also dedicated to Sharron Brooks, super reader and avid
supporter of The Levanthria series. Who sadly gained their
angel wings during the finalising of this story.

"And it is my belief that you're not truly gone, for as long as the
hearts of our children beats, I believe you will always live on,"
The Ballad Of The Borag-I
250KR

I

shenrock Hollow, a stark yet striking expanse nestled in the heart of the rugged obsidian mountain range, was home to the fierce Firetusk Clan. The village, an intricate network of caves and dwellings hewn from the mountainside, was as formidable as the Orcs who resided within.

Dotted with spires of weathered stone, the Hollow reached up from the earth like a gnarled hand, its ashen hues a stark contrast against the cerulean sky. Natural fortifications, the jagged cliffs surrounding the village, seemed to bristle with defiance, warding off those who dared to encroach upon the Orcish domain.

A narrow, winding path cut through the inhospitable terrain, the only route leading to the village. It was strewn with jagged rocks and boulders, evidence of the tumultuous geological past. The path echoed the relentless determination and tenacity of the Firetusk Clan, a tribute to their warrior spirit.

Within the Hollow, the dwellings of the Firetusk Clan were carved from the mountainside, their entrances marked by great, rune-inscribed boulders. The dwellings themselves were labyrinthine, designed to confuse and deter potential attackers. A myriad of tunnels led to different chambers, each serving a distinct purpose: communal halls for feasting and storytelling, weapon smithies, and personal abodes.

The heart of the Hollow was the Great Hall, a colossal cavern where the clan's leader, Braka-I, held counsel. The cavern's high ceiling was stained black from centuries of fire smoke, and an imposing stone chair, adorned with intricate carvings and beastly motifs, sat at the far end, serving as the leader's throne.

Amidst the harshness of the landscape, life thrived. Stout, broad-leafed vegetation clung to the mountainside, stubbornly persisting against the biting winds. Hardy mountain goats nimbly traversed the cliffs, and a clear, icy stream cut through the Hollow, providing the villagers with fresh water.

In the evening, the Hollow would resonate with the sounds of the Firetusk Clan: the rhythmic pounding of the smithy, the low hum of Orcish chants, and the crackle of fires. The air would be rich with the scent of roasting meats and the tang of metalwork, the lifeblood of the warrior clan. And amidst it all, a single, melodious note would often pierce the night, the sweet strumming of a lute: the anomaly of the Hollow, the bard named Borag-I – or Bo, as he preferred to be known.

In one of the furthest reaches of Ashenrock Hollow, tucked away in an alcove of the mountain, lay a dwelling markedly different from the rest. At the heart of this room, an oversized bed hewn from solid rock dominated the space. The sheets were a medley of animal hides, and strewn across them, like a fallen tree, was Bo.

The morning light spilled through the narrow aperture of his cave dwelling, casting long shadows over the room. The air was thick with the earthy scent of moss and the faint smell of last night's fire. In stark contrast to his robust Orcish build, Bo lay sprawled across his bed in a state of complete tranquillity. His massive feet dangled off the end, his toenails resembling small, jagged pebbles. The faint, rhythmic snoring that filled the room was barely audible over the distant clanging of the smithy.

Instead of battle scars, his fingers bore callouses from strumming the strings of his beloved lute. Instead of weapons, musical notes and lyrics were scattered across his bedside table.

Amidst the serenity of the dawn, Bo was lost in a world of dreams. His massive chest rose and fell rhythmically as he slumbered, the soft hum of a melody escaping his lips. He was dreaming about a song, his nimble fingers plucking at the strings of his lute, the notes forming a beautiful lullaby that made the stars dance in the night sky. The tune wrapped around him like a comforting blanket, filling his sleep with tranquillity.

Suddenly, the peaceful humming was disrupted by a loud, persistent knocking. The sound ricocheted off the stone walls of his dwelling, shattering the tranquillity like a boulder crashing into a serene pond. Bo jolted awake, his eyes snapping open to the dim light of the early morning. His dream melody, disrupted by the abrupt intrusion, faded into the silence, leaving him disoriented and a touch irritated at the unwelcome interruption.

Still dazed and sluggish from the abrupt awakening, Bo swung his legs over the edge of his bed, miscalculating the distance to the ground. In a tumultuous cascade of flailing limbs and disoriented grunts, he tumbled out of bed, his massive Orcish frame crashing onto the cold, hard floor. The echo of the thunderous thud reverberated through his hut, rattling the wooden frame of his bedside table. It teetered precariously before toppling over, sending a clutter of objects scattering across the stone floor.

In the midst of the chaos, Bo found himself entangled in his yakula fur sheet. The thick, heavy fur was twisted around his limbs in a cocoon of confusion. Despite the situation, Bo lay sprawled on the floor, the soft fur a stark contrast to the cold stone beneath him, a bewildered expression etched on his face as he tried to untangle himself.

Suddenly, a gruff voice shouted through the wooden door, "Bo, you're late! You've overslept!" The voice was unmistakably Orcish, deep and gravelly, like two stones grinding against each other. It was a voice seasoned by years of shouting commands on the battlefield and negotiating in the tribal council. The tone was stern, carrying an undercurrent of authority and impatience, but also a subtle hint of fond exasperation. It was a voice that was all too familiar to Bo, a voice that had reprimanded, guided, and also comforted him over the years.

Bo's pointed ears, a signature trait of his Orcish lineage, twitched in annoyance at Gorog-Thu's persistent knocking. "Curses!" His voice echoed in the small confines of his room, the word holding enough surprise and annoyance to startle a sparrow from its nest. The tall Orc sprang from his bed like a coiled spring unbound.

Standing at a height towering above the average human, Bo was an impressive sight. His body was sculpted with lean muscles, forged through years of mandatory clan training and the physically demanding lifestyle of his tribe. His long black hair, untamed and wild, cascaded down to his broad shoulders, resembling the tumultuous rapids of the River Krusk.

With a groan, Bo lumbered towards the door, his bare feet thudding against the packed earth floor. He unlatched the rough wooden door and swung it open, revealing the figure of his best friend on the other side.

Gorog-Thu stood there, his usually cheerful face etched with a panicked expression. He was shorter than Bo, though not by much, and his skin was a paler shade of green, bordering on a rustic brown.

"Bo, we need to hurry!" he urged, his voice tense.

His most noticeable feature was the gleaming metal hoop piercing one of his upward curving, tusked teeth. It was a symbol of his success in the Rite of the Firetusk, the clan's traditional trial of strength and bravery. Every Orc in the Firetusk Clan had to face this trial upon reaching maturity, a test that signified their transition into adulthood and the warrior ranks.

It was the very trial that Bo had overslept for, the thought of which sent a jolt of anxiety through his veins.

"I'm coming, I'm coming," Bo replied, his voice still thick with sleep. His hands ran through his tousled hair in a futile attempt to tame the unruly black strands. A yawn escaped him, his pointed ears twitching slightly. Despite the urgency of the situation, there was a languid grace to his movements, a rhythm that was more akin to a leisurely dance than the hurried preparation for a fierce trial. One that he really did not want to attend.

Gorog-Thu sighed, the hoop in his tusk glinting in the morning sun as he spoke. "Need I remind you that you have to pass this trial if you are to become part of the Firetusk

Clan? You've already been given more chances to pass than others in the tribe," he said, his voice tinged with a mix of concern and frustration. His eyes bore into Bo's, conveying the gravity of the situation.

Bo flashed his friend a reassuring smile, his sharp teeth standing out starkly against his vibrant green skin. "Relax, Gorog," he said, the corners of his eyes crinkling as his smile widened. "Everything will work out." His statement was simple, delivered with an air of calm confidence. Bo's felt optimistic, he couldn't understand why everyone in the Fire Tusk clan was so serious all of the time.

"There is a fine line between confidence and arrogance," Gorog retorted, his brows furrowed in despair as he shook his head at his friend's nonchalance. "How can you be so relaxed, Bo? You talk like the consequences of failing do not trouble you."

"I won't fail this time, mate," Bo assured him. "And don't worry too much. My mum wouldn't dare kick her favourite son out of the tribe." There was a spark of mischief in his words, as Bo quickly stuffed his feet into his worn leather boots.

Gorog's face turned even more serious, concern etching deep lines on his young features. "Except, you're not your mum's favourite," he said, his voice taking on a graver tone.

As Gorog mentioned Krag-I, Bo's mind couldn't help but wander to his older brother, as perfect of an orc of the Firetusk Clan's might and honour. His very name stirred tales of valour and glory within the hearts of their people. Casting a mountain of a shadow which Bo had lived under his whole life.

Krag-I, the Fire Born, was a warrior unlike any other. From a young age, he'd been the embodiment of the clan's strength and prowess. His feats in battle were the stuff of legends, passed down in hushed whispers around the campfire, inspiring the young and earning the respect of the old.

He had led the clan to victory against a marauding band of gnolls when he was barely past his youth, a feat that had earned him his title. His courage in the face of danger and his unwavering leadership had turned the tide of a battle that should have been a loss.

Then, there was the time he'd single-handedly slain a rampaging hill giant that had threatened their livestock. Using only his wits and his trusty battle-axe, he'd managed to take down the giant, protecting their livelihood and securing their survival for another harsh winter.

Each tale of Krag-I's heroics was one that added to his skill and bravery, but to Bo, they were also constant reminders of the shadow cast by his older brother, a shadow that seemed to grow longer with each passing day. The contrast between his brother's accomplishments and his own aspirations to become a bard couldn't be more stark. But Bo wouldn't let these thoughts deter him; he was determined to carve out his own path, one note at a time.

"Come, Gorag," Bo began, his voice a calm, steady drumbeat against the rhythm of the morning. "The morning brings with it a fresh day, one that will favour me."

As if to underscore his words, Bo took a deep breath, the crisp morning air filling his lungs and adding a tangible weight to his resolution. He reached out, placing his large, calloused hands on Gorag's narrower shoulders. The contact was as much for Bo's reassurance as it was for his friend's.

"Today," Bo said, "will be a good day."

Unlike the hardened warriors of the Firetusk Clan, Bo

held a secret, a longing that separated him from his kin. He was an Orc of the Firetusk Clan, true he was not yet initiated and yes, he would be bound by blood and tradition once he completed his trial, but his heart was drawn to a different path. As Bo grabbed his leather gloves and followed a grumpy Gorag outside into the morning sun, a fresh knot of nerves began to form in his stomach with his trial looming over him yet again.

He loved his tribe, revered the strength and unity that defined them, respected the traditions that had held them together for generations. But, deep within him, Bo yearned for something else, something his kin might not understand.

Bo was not like the other Orcs. He didn't find joy in the clash of steel, didn't revel in the thrill of battle. Violence was an innate part of his culture, yet it held no allure for him. The thought of hurting others, of inflicting pain, was a concept that sat uneasily in his mind.

His heart, instead, was filled with melody and rhythm. The thrumming of the drums of war was replaced with the strumming of a lute, the gruff battle cries substituted with soothing ballads. His warrior's spirit was tempered by a bard's soul.

The truth was, Bo had no desire to be a fearsome warrior, to follow in the footsteps of his ancestors. No, Bo wanted to sing. He wanted to be a bard, to tell stories of his people through song, to convey their strength, their spirit, their honour, through his music. His was a desire that would set him apart, a dream that would make him an outcast in his own tribe. But it was a path he was willing to tread, a destiny he was ready to embrace.

2

The journey through Ashenrock Hollow led Bo and Gorag to the hallowed grounds of the trial pits. These were no ordinary pits; they were an arena crafted from the rugged heart of the land, a hollowed-out basin embraced by the surrounding hills. The earth here bore the scars of countless trials and battles, each mark a story etched into the very fabric of the Firetusk Clan.

Sentinels of stone, grand statues of past Orc warriors, stood tall around the perimeter, their fierce expressions immortalised in the weathered rock. Their eyes, devoid of life yet brimming with spirit, watched over the arena, a storm filled atmosphere steeped with the clan's glorious history and the legacy its members strived to uphold– a legacy that felt heavy whenever Bo tried to imagine bearing it.

Inside the arena, the ground was an unsettling tapestry of crushed bones, each a remnant of a trial past.

No, Bo thought. These were not just remnants but tributes, bone shrines to the triumphant and the fallen, a reminder of the stakes that hung in the balance for him today.

A massive gathering of Orcs encircled the pit, their muscular forms lit by the dancing flames of scattered fires. The air vibrated with their anticipation, a collective heartbeat that pulsed through the arena. The trial was not just a test; it was a spectacle, a celebration of strength and courage deeply ingrained in their culture.

As Bo and Gorag emerged into the firelit circle, a murmur rippled through the crowd. Their lateness had not gone unnoticed, and a sea of glowing eyes appraised them with a blend of curiosity and judgement. Yet, Bo stood tall, his broad shoulders relaxed, his face calm. Beside him, Gorag seemed more affected by the crowd, his eyes skittering nervously over the faces. Still, his posture was firm, his loyalty to Bo evident in his determination.

At the heart of the bone-littered pit, they faced the expectant crowd, the echoes of past trials whispering around them.

At the epicentre of the pit stood a figure of undeniable command, her presence an imposing beacon amid the sea of warriors. Braka-I, the Firetusk Clan leader.

Bo's mother.

Her expression was a storm of suppressed frustration, eyes like glowing embers fixated on the latecomers. She was a force to reckon with, her reputation as a seasoned warrior and fair leader preceding her. Yet at this moment, she was a mother less than impressed with her son's tardiness. Her eyes gazed down on him, adding further weight on his shoulders, judging and expectant. In this moment he wished he could be more like his big brother and to make her proud.

Cloaked in the dusky glow of the firelight, Braka-I's

imposing silhouette seemed to command the pit. She was encased in a striking suit of bone-mail armour, each piece meticulously crafted and imbued with the spirits of ancestral warriors. The armour was more than protection—it was a symbol of her authority, her strength, her lineage.

As her gaze met Bo's, there was an undeniable spark of challenge in her eyes, a silent demand for him to prove himself. Today was not just another trial; it was a test of his commitment to the clan, to his lineage, and to her.

The matriarch's hair, a cascade of midnight black, was plaited tightly and tied back, revealing a face lined with the wisdom of years. From her lower jaw jutted two impressive tusks, filed to sharp points. Each tusk was filled with rings from top to bottom, a mark of her achievements and a visual chronicle of her leadership.

To her right stood Bo's elder brother, Krag-I the Fire Born. He was a mountain of an Orc, hulking and broad shouldered, his body a tangible manifestation of years of relentless training and combat. His arms, thick as tree trunks, were crossed over his massive chest, the muscles rippling beneath his skin like an agitated sea. His stern face was a mirror of their mother's, etched with a seriousness that seemed as perennial as the age-old stones of Ashenrock Hollow.

His tusks, just as impressive as their mother's, were adorned with rings. Each represented a trial overcome, a victory won. They pierced his bone tusks, fewer in number than Braka-I's but nonetheless significant.

Bo's gaze lingered on Krag-I, his contempt simmering beneath the surface of his usual easy-going demeanour. Krag-I was everything Bo wasn't: the warrior, the prodigy, the next-in-line. He was the embodiment of the Firetusk Clan's ideals, a living symbol of their traditions and beliefs. The perfect son in their mother's eyes, the perfect successor to the clan's leadership.

The silence was broken by Krag's voice, deep and resounding like the low rumble of a distant thunderstorm. "You are late, Borag-I," he stated, the words slicing through the quiet morning air with an edge of disapproval.

Bo's lips curled into a rare scowl as he met his brother's stern gaze. "Just Bo will do," he responded breezily. His words hung in the air, a rebellious echo bouncing off the surrounding bone shrines, the audacity of his casualness reverberating through the silent crowd.

Upon hearing Bo's defiant response, Krag-I's eyes bulged in surprise. A surge of irritation swiftly replaced his momentary shock, causing his nostrils to flare akin to a mighty beast disturbed in its lair.

The commanding, thunderous voice of Braka-I reverberated through the trial pits, silencing the murmurs of the onlooking Orcs. "You stand on sacred ground, in our ancestral trial pits!" she barked, her fierce eyes locked onto Bo's defiant form. "You will be addressed by your true name, the name bestowed upon you at birth. The name I gave you, both as your mother and as leader of the Firetusk Clan." Her voice echoed around the pit, carrying the weight and authority of generations of Orcish tradition. "Borag-I!"

Braka continued, her voice ringing out strong and clear over the gathered Orcish spectators. "You have been summoned here today" – she cast a disapproving glance in Bo's direction – "albeit late, to participate in the Rite of Passage. This rite is a sacred tradition of the mighty Firetusk Clan. A tradition that you, Borag-I, will undertake this day."

With her words, a pulse of primal energy surged through the crowd, culminating in a deafening roar that echoed through the pits, resonating off the bone shrines and statues of past warriors. The sheer force of the united voices of the Firetusk Clan shook the ground beneath their feet, making the air itself tremble. This eruption of raw, wild emotion reached into the very core of Bo's heart, shaking him to his roots. It was a vivid, powerful reminder of the weight of the tradition he was about to undertake, a rite so deeply ingrained in the identity of his tribe. This was not merely a trial, but a defining moment that would shape his place in the clan, and for a fleeting moment, Bo could feel the gravity of it all. The temptation to run, gripped his chest, stifling a breath as his heart beat intensified. He could feel the grip of panic squezzing him even harder, the noise of the crowd cheering became an echoed cheer in the back of his mind as the the pit started to spin around him. A wave of different shades of green surrounded him as everything span for a quick moment before he noticed Gorag in the crowd. Seeing his friend somehow centred him, it grounded him and with a reassuring nod he pushed down the temptation to flee as best a she could. That did not mean that it wasn't however still present. Simmering underneath the service like stew in a pot.

As the roars of the crowd continued to echo in the trial pits, Braka raised her hands, a command for silence that was instantly obeyed. The cacophony died down to a hushed anticipation, all eyes turning to their clan leader.

"Today, you will face a creature handpicked by our very own Beast Master, Viran-Ux," Braka-I announced, turning to gesture towards a monolithic figure standing at the edge of the crowd.

The name stirred a fresh wave of cheers from the clan

13

for the scarred titan whose reputation was built on his uncanny ability to tame and command the wildest of beasts. Viran-Ux, an imposing spectacle, stood bald with a distinctive white eye – a gift from a past confrontation with a feral creature, now accentuated by a gnarly scar that tore through it. His right hand was missing, and his skin was a canvas of clawed scars.

As he lifted his remaining hand to acknowledge the clan's admiration, a sense of foreboding washed over Bo. To face one of Viran-Ux's selected creatures was a daunting prospect, one that added an entirely new dimension of dread to his impending trial.

"Today, Borag-I, you will join our ranks within the great and mighty Firetusk Clan," Braka-I proclaimed. She fixed her stern gaze upon Bo, the weight of her expectations pressing heavily upon his broad shoulders. "Failure is not an option. To do so will result in your banishment. But I need not remind you of the consequences." Her words, stark and brutal, hung in the air.

This was not uncharted territory for Bo. In fact, it was an all too familiar scenario. He had faced the trial pit four times before, each time emerging defeated, his spirit bruised but not broken. In a tribe as fierce as the Firetusk Clan, two failures typically led to banishment. But Bo, being the son of Braka-I, had been granted some leniency, an allowance born more from familial bonds than from any indulgence in weakness.

Yet as he stood there, the nervous flutter in his stomach could not be quelled. His gaze flickered to his mother, the stern clan leader, her eyes piercing as they met his. Bo swallowed hard, yet a spark of defiance remained. He was cocksure, a trait that both irritated and confounded his tribe. Despite the heavy threat of banishment, he held fast to an underlying belief that his mother, despite her harsh exterior, would never truly cast her own son out into the cold, unwelcoming exile.

Standing tall in the pit, Bo's emerald eyes glistened with a cocktail of anticipation and defiance as he held the gaze of his mother and the eager crowd. His mouth curved into a self-assured grin, flaunting his pointed, ivory tusks as he boldly declared, "Bring on the beast."

The crowd's deafening roar echoed off the stone walls of the pit as Bo's daring proclamation stirred their spirits. In the midst of this primal cacophony, Gorog moved closer to Bo.

Placing a heavy hand on Bo's shoulder, he leaned in, his voice firm amidst the uproarious crowd. "Good luck, Bo. May Xurud look down on you with favour."

With a reassured nod and an easy-going smile that seemed to shrug off the gravity of the situation, Bo responded, "I'll be fine, Gorog. What's the worst that can happen?" In that moment, Bo tried not to look at the bones that littered the pit around him, reminding himself that for an Orc, there were worse things than death.

Gorog exhaled a heavy sigh and shook his head. He clapped Bo's shoulder one last time before stepping back, leaving his friend to face the impending trial alone.

Meanwhile, Braka-I and Krag-I silently retreated from the centre of the pit to join the throng of spectators. No words of wisdom or encouragement were proffered, the weight of the unspoken expectations hanging in the air.

Bo watched them walk away, a peculiar mix of resignation and determination settling over him. His heart pounded in his chest like the tribal drums on the eve of a great hunt. This was it. Once again, he was alone, facing the judgement of the pit, the judgement of the Firetusk Clan.

The Beast Master, Viran-Ux, moved towards a rusted, hefty chain attached to the gate of the beast pen. With a mighty heave, he pulled, the gate protesting with a grating screech as it was hoisted upwards. As the dark maw of the beast pen was revealed, Bo found his heart pounding against his ribcage with an intensity that echoed in his ears.

He had been here before – four times, to be precise. Each time, a different beast had emerged from that darkness, a new horror designed to test his courage. He had faced the clawed fury of a skragg, the venomous wrath of a blight serpent, the crushing force of an ironhide grunn, and the relentless pursuit of a bloodfang worg. Each time, he had chosen flight over fight, self-preservation over a mindless display of bravery.

Now, as the pen's gate creaked fully open, Bo's breath hitched in anticipation as he waited to see what monster had been chosen for him this time. His green eyes hardened, the memory of previous failures fuelling his resolve. This time, he would not run. This time, he would face whatever horror lurked in the shadows.

A low, guttural growl echoed from the depths of the beast pen, a primal sound that sent a shiver coursing down Bo's spine. His hands clenched into fists at his sides, his knuckles turning a shade paler under the strain. The growl was met with an excited ripple of anticipation from the gathered Orcs, their eagerness for the impending combat palpable in the electrified air.

To his side, a small arsenal of Orcish weapons lay strewn about, their wickedly sharp edges glinting menacingly in the morning light. They were a variety of brutal tools; bone-hilted swords, spiked maces, and jagged-edged axes – each one designed to deal deadly blows to any adversary.

Yet, their placement was no mere coincidence. Purposefully left right next to the pen, they were designed to draw the initiate towards the impending danger, to coerce them into the heart of the action, into the maw of the beast.

For Bo, however, this was a prospect he was keen on avoiding. He had no interest in charging headfirst into a melee, no desire to spill blood for the sake of it. His heart yearned for melody, not for battle cries, and his hands longed for the strings of his guitar, not the cold hilt of a sword. Yet, he knew he had to face this challenge head-on, for his tribe, for his mother, but most importantly, for himself. If Bo could pass his trial with honor and bravery, he might finally gain the respect of his tribe, and with that, a leniency that could permit him to chase his dream of being a bard.

Rising from the depths of the pen was a creature known as a leocentaur. Its body was as robust and graceful as a horse's, covered in a tawny coat of fur. Its head, however, was that of a lion's, complete with a wild mane and a mouth full of deadly, gleaming teeth.

Its eyes were a haunting amber, flickering with a predatory hunger that seemed to bore into Bo's very soul. The creature's strong, horse-like legs ended in lion-like paws, each with sharp, retractable claws that scratched against the ground. A tail, more akin to a lion's, flicked restlessly behind it, the tufted end swishing in anticipation of the forthcoming battle.

Protruding from its lion-head were two large, twisted horns, their ivory hue contrasting sharply against the tawny fur, their pointed tips gleaming ominously, prepared to skewer and slay with ruthless efficiency.

Not what Bo wanted to face.

As the beast made its presence known, a primal terror

welled up inside Bo. He was no stranger to these trials, and yet, the sight of the creature, its predatory eyes locked onto him, struck a chord of dread that rooted him to the spot. Despite the mental commands he sent to his legs, they refused to comply, frozen in place as if the ground beneath them had turned to solid ice. All his previous encounters with the beasts of the trial pit flashed before his eyes, sending a shiver down his spine. The air around him seemed to thin, making every breath a struggle. He was trapped in the beast's gaze, his body paralysed by a fear that he had never felt before.

Bo's struggle was not due to lack of physical prowess. He had spent the last twenty-five years training and preparing for combat, his body honed and ready for the challenges that the trials presented. He was a Firetusk, after all, born from a lineage of warriors whose physical might was the stuff of legends.

The battle that raged within him was far more complex. It was a clash of values, of identity. On one side, the expectations of his tribe and lineage demanded that he show his might, claim his first hoop on his tusk, and secure his place in the Firetusk Clan. He knew he had the capacity, the potential to take down the beast before him, to claim victory and honour in the eyes of his people.

On the other side, though, was a different desire, one that set him apart from his kin. Bo had no interest in fighting, no desire to harm another creature, no matter how fearsome it might be. He was not like his kin, he did not revel in combat and conquest. His heart yearned for a different path, one of harmony, not discord; of creation, not destruction.

Amidst the clamour of the crowd, a voice sliced through

the air, jolting Bo from his mental turmoil. "Do something, Bo!" Gorog-Thu pleaded.

As Bo stood there, paralysed, the crowd started to react. Laughter broke out, harsh and cruel, bouncing off the walls of the pit.

"Look at him! He's frozen!" one Orc jeered, his voice booming with mockery.

"Seems like Bo has pissed himself!" another chimed in, a malicious grin splitting his face.

Each jab stung more than the last. Despite their brutal exterior, Orcs loved a spectacle, and right now, Bo was providing them with just that.

A wave of embarrassment washed over Bo as the heat rose to his cheeks. His face flushed a deeper shade of green, and he couldn't help but feel the weight of the entire tribe's eyes upon him. Yet, despite the shame and humiliation, he remained rooted to the spot, unable to move to take a single step forward.

With a formidable roar, the leocentaur bared its teeth, its eyes ablaze with primal fury. It pawed the ground once, twice, and then exploded into a gallop. Dust billowed behind the creature, its every stride powerful and purposeful, closing the distance between it and Bo with terrifying speed.

All the while, Bo could only stand there, transfixed by the sight before him. His eyes were locked onto the leocentaur's, caught in the hypnotic gaze of the beast that was charging towards him. He could see the burning intensity in the creature's eyes, the raw, untamed power of a beast forged by nature's harshest conditions. The sight should have terrified him, spurred him into action, but it didn't. Instead, he felt a strange sense of calm washing over him, as if time had slowed down and all he could hear was the rhythmic beat of his own heart.

The world around him blurred into insignificance, the jeering crowd fading into the background. It was just him and the leocentaur now, their eyes locked in an eerie dance of life and death.

Just as the leocentaur was about to reach Bo, a blur of motion shot past him. His mother had charged into the ring, her bone-mail armour shimmering as she moved with speed and agility. Grabbing hold of the leocentaur's curled horns, she forced its head downwards, causing the creature to skid in the dust, scrambling to regain control. With a strength that could only come from years of leading the Firetusk Clan, Braka-I shifted her weight and spun around. The leocentaur, caught off guard, was sent sprawling away from Bo, a trail of dust billowing in its wake.

The crowd fell silent, their cheers and laughter abruptly cut short. All eyes were on the pit, where the leader of the Firetusk Clan had intervened to protect her son. There was an air of disbelief as the spectators watched the unfolding spectacle, their raucous jeers replaced by a stunned silence.

Reacting swiftly, Viran-Ux, the Beast Master, lunged towards the displaced leocentaur and hurled thick chains around the creature's neck. His single white eye glinted with a calculated precision as he yanked on the chains, pulling the beast off balance.

The leocentaur snarled and thrashed, but Viran-Ux stood firm. His muscles bulged, straining against the weight of the beast, yet he maintained an iron grip on the chains. The strength he displayed was colossal, dwarfing even that of the largest warriors in the clan. Bo stood, frozen to the spot, his legs paralysed with fear, as much as he willed them to move it was as though his feet were made from stone.

With a resounding roar that echoed in the pit, Viran-Ux dragged the rearing leocentaur backwards, his every movement timed to counter the beast's desperate attempts to break free. It wasn't long before he had pulled the creature back towards the pen, despite its snarling protests. The crowd watched in awed silence, their breaths held as they witnessed the sheer force of the Beast Master.

The proud leader of the Firetusk Clan now stood deflated, her imposing figure somehow diminished by Bo's lack of action.

She did not even have to speak for Bo to understand.

He had failed.

3

The laughter and jeers of his tribe strung like an open wound as Bo made his way back to his hut, but he held his head high, not letting them see his pain. In a moment of frustration, he kicked open his door, the sturdy wood splintering under his force.

The room, a familiar refuge, seemed to close in on him as he stormed in. His bed, his solitary haven, was the only welcoming sight. Without a second thought, he dove onto it, sinking into the soft yakula fur mattress. Burying his face in his pillow, he tried to banish the world outside and the disappointment that coursed through his veins. The pillow muffled his frustrated groans, providing the only comfort in this moment of utter defeat.

The sound of hesitant footfalls broke through the suffocating silence in the room.

"Are you okay, Bo?"

Gorog-Thu had followed him home.

Bo's muffled voice seeped out from beneath the pillow, thick with frustration and bitterness. "You didn't see the way she looked at me, Gorog," he growled. "The hatred in her eyes . . . It was like I was a stranger. I'm her son, not some enemy."

Then his voice grew harsher, rising in volume as he continued, "And don't get me started on Krag! I could see his smug grin plastered all over his face when I failed."

The image of his brother's self-satisfied expression at the pit was seared into his mind. "He revels in my misery, the bastard," he spat.

"What do you think will happen now, Bo?" Gorog asked, shifting uncomfortably where he stood. "You know the consequences when someone fails the trial." His voice wavered, but he kept his eyes on his friend, a glimmer of worry flickering in his otherwise sturdy gaze.

Bo sighed heavily. "I've been in this mess before, Gorog," he said, finally lifting his head to meet his friend's gaze. "She'll probably forgive me again. I'll just need to lay low for a while . . . Until the dust settles, at least."

As he said this, his mind replayed the image of his mother's face, her burning gaze seared into his memory. The disappointment, the anger – it was a sight he was all too familiar with. Yet, this time, something felt different. A cold, sinking feeling nestled itself in the pit of his stomach, a new, unwelcome guest. Was it possible that this time she meant what she said? Could she truly follow through on her threats? The thought sent a shiver down his spine, leaving him in a cold sweat despite the warmth of his room.

Gorog gave him an uncertain look, seemingly weighing his words. "You're the chieftain's son," he affirmed, scratching at his tusk nervously. "I agree, you just need to keep your head down for a few days, maybe a week." He paused, his brow furrowing as he studied Bo's face. "Or . . . even six," he added, the jest failing to completely mask his concern.

"Thank you," Bo said simply, his voice a whisper in the quiet room. Shifting his gaze, he reached forward to grab hold of the one object that always brought him comfort – his guitar.

It was an odd sight to see an Orc with such a delicate instrument, but Bo held it with a gentle care, a stark contrast to the usual roughness associated with his kind. The worn wood felt familiar and comforting under his touch, the strings cool against his fingers.

With a deep breath, he began to play. The tune was soft and melodic, the notes floating around the room in a soothing rhythm. His fingers danced over the strings with an ease that came from years of practice, each strum a sign of his dedication.

Bo allowed his mind to focus solely on the music, the familiar notes helping to calm the turmoil of his thoughts. He adjusted his grip, refining a couple of notes, his heart starting to sync with the rhythm of the song. The room filled with the melodic sound, his worries momentarily fading away.

As Bo continued to strum the strings of his guitar, the tension seemed to melt from his body. The rhythmical patterns he was forming were like a salve to his soul, each note soothing the turmoil of the day's events. His fingers danced over the strings with practiced precision, plucking a melody that was as familiar to him as his own heartbeat.

Gorog, who had been watching Bo from across the room, was tapping his fingers against his leg in time with the music.

For a moment, they were simply two friends sharing a moment of peace in the midst of chaos. The more Bo played, the more the room seemed to hum with a relaxed energy, the music offering a temporary reprieve from their worries.

Bo took a deep breath and began to sing:

"In the pit of trials, young Bo stood,
Faced a beast, did as best he could."

His voice, strong and melodic, carried the emotions of his day. He strummed the strings of his guitar with more conviction, the music mirroring his growing defiance.

"His heart, it roared, yet his body froze,
In the face of danger, that's how it goes."

The room echoed with the rhythm, his words painting vivid pictures of his ordeal. He could see Gorog's eyes soften, the song clearly resonating with him.

"Mocking eyes, they pierced his soul,
His spirit crushed, paying the toll."

The frustration in his voice was palpable. His fingers danced on the strings, striking a chord that reverberated within his heart.

. . .

"Yet, in his heart, a song remains,
In spite of failure, despite the pains."

As the song came to an end, a sense of peace washed over Bo. He looked at Gorog, a small smile tugging at the corners of his mouth. This was him, his true self. He wasn't meant to be a warrior, he was meant to be a bard, a storyteller. Music was his real tribe, and his guitar, his true weapon.

His music wasn't just a tool for expression; it was his coping mechanism, his therapy. With each note that flowed from his guitar, the angst and pent up frustration seemed to lessen, becoming less concrete, less imposing. His humiliation, once as rigid and imposing as a wall, now ebbed away like the tide, leaving behind a calmness that surprised him.

And as the last note of his guitar faded into silence, Bo found himself in a state of tranquillity. The memories of the trial, the jeering crowd, his brother's smug face, and his mother's disappointment – they all seemed distant now, like shadows retreating in the light of his music.

Yes, he had failed the trials, but in this moment, playing his guitar and singing his heart out, Bo felt like he had won something much more important. He had won back his peace.

The soothing echo of the final chord was still lingering in the air when Bo's gaze drifted up to the entrance of his hut. All the tranquillity he had found in his music vanished as quickly as a light gust of wind extinguishes a candle.

There, filling the doorway with his imposing stature,

stood Krag-I, his face twisted into an expression of pure fury. The comfortable atmosphere in the room shifted in an instant, replaced with a tense silence that made the air feel heavy and suffocating once more. The calm sea that Bo's music had summoned was now replaced with an impending storm, and Bo could already feel the first drops of rain.

Without any warning, Krag lunged forward, seizing Gorog by the scruff of his neck. His grip was iron-clad, the raw power in his muscles evident. With a swift, jerky motion, he tossed Gorog outside the room.

His voice, when he spoke, was low and threatening, a barely restrained growl. "Leave while you still can."

Gorog stumbled out, casting one last worried glance at Bo before he disappeared from sight. Krag then pivoted, his hard gaze returning to Bo. His icy stare was penetrating, seeming to bore into Bo's very soul. The room fell silent, the tension thick enough to cut with a knife.

With a stern, unyielding expression, Krag said, "You bring great shame to our family, to the Firetusk Clan."

"If that's all you've come here to say, you may as well just leave," Bo retorted with a defiant glint in his eyes. "I'd rather spend my time with someone who possesses the intellect required for meaningful conversation."

Krag's nostrils flared wide, rage billowing from his gaze. It was a silent but potent warning that caused Bo to reconsider his words, wondering if he'd perhaps prodded the beast a tad too far.

"Leave me be, Krag," Bo said, his voice taking on a tone of weary dismissal. "I'd rather not have company right now, least of all yours."

With a self-satisfied air, Krag tilted his head, his eyes

gleaming with triumph. "In exile, you'll find all the space you could ever desire."

Rolling his eyes, Bo gestured towards the door. "I don't have time for this, Krag."

With an agility that contradicted his hulking frame, Krag swiftly gripped Bo by the scruff of his neck, hoisting him up until they were eye to eye.

His foul breath washed over Bo, who managed to retort with a cheeky grin, "Ever heard of a tusk brush, brother?"

Krag's response to the quip was a roar of pure rage. With a swift, powerful motion, he flung Bo with an astonishing force, causing him to crash through the wooden wall of his room. Bo flew through the air, his body careening off the rough dirt outside and skidding across the gravelly ground in a cloud of dust and debris.

Reeling from the sudden violent flight, Bo found himself disoriented, the world around him spinning in a haze of confusion. He heaved, a rough cough escaping from his lungs as he struggled to regain his bearings. As the dust began to settle, it slowly dawned on him that he wasn't alone. A group of Orcs from his tribe had formed a crowd around the house. Their faces reflected a strange mix of curiosity and anticipation. Among them, standing at the front, was his mother, Braka-I. Her stern face was unreadable, but there was a certain tension in her stance that worried Bo.

Through the settling cloud of dust and the jagged remnants of his once intact wall, the hulking silhouette of Krag loomed ominously. The colossal Orc stood there, triumphant, holding something in his massive, clenched fist. As the dust cleared, the reality hit Bo like a punch in the gut. Krag was holding his cherished guitar, the instrument that offered him solace and comfort in his most dire moments. The sight of his brother wielding his precious possession ignited a fresh wave of horror in Bo's heart.

Krag's voice rang out, clear and intimidating in the sudden quiet. "I found this worm" – he gestured at Bo with a dismissive flick of his hand – "not in turmoil at failing yet another trial. Not clamouring for forgiveness for bringing shame to the Firetusk Clan."

The muscular Orc towered over the scene, his broad shoulders backlit by the setting sun, casting an imposing shadow that fell across the gathered crowd. His eyes, burning with an inferno of contempt and rage, bored into Bo's.

"Instead," Krag sneered, "he was playing music and singing with this blasted thing." He held up the guitar for the crowd to see, his fingers coiled around it like a vice. The guitar looked absurdly small, almost fragile, in his immense grasp.

Driven by a desperate need to save his prized instrument, Bo sprang to his feet and hurled himself at Krag. His fingers clawed at his brother's hand, trying to pry the guitar free. But Krag's grip was unyielding, as solid and immovable as a mountain. With a swift, dismissive shove, Krag sent Bo sprawling back onto the ground.

Krag then casually tossed the guitar towards their mother. The instrument skidded across the gravelly surface, throwing up a cloud of dust before coming to a halt right in front of her feet. The strings hummed a mournful note, distorted and discordant.

Braka-I's gaze flickered between the guitar and Bo, her expression an unreadable mask. Her eyes, however, bore a clear message of disapproval. As she looked at Bo, her gaze bore into him, sending a chill down his spine. It was a look he had seen before, a look of disappointment that cut deeper than any Orcish blade.

"Is what your brother says true, Borag-I?" she asked, her gaze never wavering from Bo's.

With his heart pounding, Bo rose from the ground, dusting himself off before he turned to face his mother. "I . . . I'm sorry, Mother," he stammered, desperation seeping into his voice. "I didn't mean to fail, I promise, I'll do better next time." His eyes were pleading, searching his mother's face for a hint of leniency or understanding.

With a thunderous growl that echoed throughout the clearing, she proclaimed, "You bring great shame upon our glorious Firetusk Clan, Borag-I. I have afforded you opportunities to pass our sacred trials and ascend our ranks, opportunities that no other Orc in this tribe has been given. And each time, you have spat on these chances, tossed them back in my face, in the face of our entire tribe."

Her voice hardened. "In accordance with our ancient Bone Laws, Borag-I, I hereby banish you from the Firetusk Clan. May you wander the wilderness until you find the purpose that eludes you here."

Inside, Bo's mind was a tumult. Over the years, the threat of banishment had hung over him like a storm cloud, but he had always seen it as a distant thunder, a mere rumbling that would never break. His mother, despite her stern demeanour, had always shown him leniency – or so he thought. He had convinced himself that she would never actually cast him out, that blood was thicker than the clan's laws. Yet here he was, standing in the cold reality of exile.

His mother had actually followed through on her threats. It was something he had never truly prepared himself for.

"Mother, p-please," Bo stammered. His knees threatened to buckle, his heart pounded in his chest. He turned his pleading eyes to his brother. "Krag?" he implored, but the stoic face of his elder sibling held no mercy.

He spun around, his gaze darting across the faces of his kin, searching for a hint of sympathy, a sign of support. "Please," his voice echoed across the silent crowd. "Don't do this. I . . . I can do better. I p-promise." Each word was a plea, an oath he was desperate to make good on. But his pleas were met with hard faces and closed hearts, leaving him feeling more isolated than ever.

Bo's eyes found Gorog in the crowd.

His friend, always steadfast, always there for him through thick and thin, looked stricken. Gorog could not meet his gaze, his shoulders slumped, his head bowed. He was powerless in this situation; no amount of camaraderie or pleas could influence the chieftain's decision. This silent rejection struck Bo like a physical blow.

A wave of regret flooded Bo's consciousness. He wished he could have been different, wished he could have been the Orc his family and his tribe expected him to be. If only he could have suppressed his distaste for violence, if only he could have silenced the melodies in his heart and quieted the songs in his soul. But it was too late now.

He had squandered his chances, lost in his own world of melodies and dreams, oblivious to the realities of his world. Now, the repercussions of his choices were all too clear as he stood on the precipice of exile, surrounded by the cold, indifferent faces of his clan. His heart ached with regret, with a yearning for a past he could not change and a future he could not avoid.

In this moment, the crowd of watching Orcs became a blur to Bo. An undulating wall of all shades of green, from the palest of limes to the darkest of forest hues, swam before his eyes. Their jeers and scornful remarks tore through the air, their long-suppressed frustration at the leniency he had been granted now spilling forth. As the world spun dizzyingly around him, the vibrancy of the Orcish throng was a disorienting storm of colour. His heart pounded in his chest as the weight of their disdain pressed heavily upon him, the crushing reality of his predicament threatening to pull him under.

In this moment, Bo's world was reeling. The jeers from the crowd, the scornful gaze of his mother, and the smug satisfaction on his brother's face coalesced into a whirling vortex of stress and humiliation. A sickening knot twisted in the pit of his stomach, threatening to surge up his throat. He clamped his jaws together, fighting the wretched gag reflex that bubbled up his oesophagus. His mouth tasted of bile and defeat as he struggled to swallow down the instinctual urge to vomit, his body's physical response to the sheer terror and betrayal he was enduring.

Mocking cries erupted from the crowd of Orcs, their voices uniting in a dissonant symphony of scorn.

"Can't even accept exile with honour!" one Orc hollered, his voice a raw taunt in the harsh morning air.

Another Orc, large and brutish, spat on the ground. "Shame!" he growled, the word laced with disgust.

Soon the word echoed around him. "Shame! Shame! SHAME!" The crowd's roars seemed to become one, a single unified voice, their collective scorn echoing loudly against the stone walls of their encampment. The discordant uproar was deafening, each utterance a spear thrust into Bo's already shattered pride.

His mother, Braka-I, glanced at the crowd berating her son and lowered her head in shame, her face a mask of disappointment and heartache. Her gaze then shifted to

Bo's guitar lying on the ground in front of her, and her expression changed in an instant. Her face contorted with anger, her lips curling into a snarl.

With a voice like the crack of a whip, Braka-I bellowed, "You show more respect for this . . . *thing*" – her words sliced through the baying crowd – "than you do for the Firetusk Clan!"

Her hand lifted and the guitar rose high in the air, catching the light of the late morning sun. Her expression remained as stern and unyielding as granite.

Desperate, Bo cried out, "Mother, please! Don't do this!"

In the penetrating gaze that met his, Bo found no trace of the nurturing mother he'd once known. The eyes staring back were stern, unyielding, void of familial affection. They were the eyes of a chieftain who had made a grave decision.

Without a shred of hesitation, his mother brought the guitar crashing down onto the rocky earth. The violent impact severed the neck from the body, leaving the once cherished instrument in a splintered ruin, held together only by its strings. She then hurled the shattered relic towards Bo.

A guttural, agonised "No!" tore from Bo's throat as he watched the final remnants of his cherished guitar – a relic of his vanished father – skid across the gravel. That instrument was far more than a tool for melody; it was a cherished keepsake, a tangible connection to the paternal figure who had disappeared into the vast plains of Anashtarr. To see it broken and discarded like this was akin to losing a loved one all over again.

"Borag-I," his mother said with a voice as cold as the northern frost, "you are exiled, never to return to Ashenrock

Hollow." Her gaze was like a dagger, sharp and merciless, as she motioned to the guards.

Two burly Orcs promptly moved forward, their heavy hands clamping onto Bo's upper arms. Their iron grips left no room for resistance, and Bo was forcibly dragged away from his home, his tribe, and the life he had known. He glanced back over his shoulder, his eyes lingering on the shattered remains of his guitar, the splintered embodiment of his dreams.

4

B o's body jostled and skidded across the rocky terrain as he was roughly flung forward by the Orcish guards. The village of Ashenrock Hollow, once his home, was now a fading image in the distance. His rear collided painfully with the stony ground, his teeth clattering from the impact. He was discarded like unwanted refuse, tossed aside with no more regard than a piece of garbage.

One of the burly Orc guards sneered down at Bo, a cruel grin splitting his coarse face. "Enjoy your new life, you runt," he jeered, his voice grating like stone on steel. "No longer will you taint our tribe with your musk." He let out a gruff laugh that echoed off the barren landscape.

To Bo, the words spoken by the Orc were nothing more than a muffled echo, his head feeling as if it was submerged under water. His mind was reeling, caught in a whirlwind of disbelief and despair. This all felt like a surreal nightmare, a wild dream from which he expected to awaken at any moment. Reality seemed to ebb and flow around him, the harsh jeers and the barren landscape fading into a hazy blur. It was as if he was standing on the outside, looking in on someone else's life.

The discordant twang of Bo's guitar strings resonated through the air as the other Orc flung it haphazardly towards him. It was a dismal, unsettling sound, like the death knell of his old life. The Orc's gruff voice cut through the haze, a harsh taunt against the backdrop of his spiralling thoughts. "Good luck saving that!" he sneered, the scorn in his voice palpable.

The two Orcs, with their malicious grins still plastered on their faces, turned their backs on Bo, walking off without sparing him another glance. Their laughter echoed in the silent expanse, leaving Bo alone and destitute in the desolate, barren wastelands of the Gorgoroth Flats.

This was it. The realisation dawned on Bo as the echoes of the Orc's laughter faded into the distance. He was exiled, banished from the only home he had ever known. As he sat there, alone in the desolate Gorgoroth Flats, he couldn't help but think of the small, silly things he'd miss about the Firetusk Clan.

No more races on the back of the young gronnlings, he thought, a pang of nostalgia hitting him as he remembered the wind rushing past him, the thrill of competition coursing through his veins.

No more late-night feasts around the fire with stories and laughter filling the air.

His heart ached at the thought of the camaraderie, the sense of belonging that he'd taken for granted.

No more training sessions with Krag, the gruelling but rewarding experience of honing one's skills.

Bo realised that he'd even miss his brother's stern face, the feeling of accomplishment when he managed to land a hit.

And no more Blood Moon Festival, the most anticipated event in the clan's calendar each year. The memory of the vibrant celebrations, the music, and the dancing seemed like a cruel joke now.

With an aching heart, Bo reached out for the remnants of his guitar, cradling it in his arms as though it were a fragile infant. He carefully brushed away the dust from its splintered body, his rough fingers tracing over the familiar contours, a sombre silence wrapping around him.

The sight of his cherished instrument, now reduced to a mere shadow of its former self, was a cruel reflection of his own state. Stripped of his identity, his home, his clan, he was as broken as the guitar he held in his arms.

Tears welled up in his eyes, blurring his vision. They streamed down his face, carving a path over the rough, green skin. His fingers tightened around the guitar, the usually sturdy wood creaking ominously under his grip.

He bowed his head, his long, unkempt hair forming a curtain around him, shielding his sorrow from the world. For a moment, he allowed himself to grieve, to mourn the loss of his past life, his home, and the comfort of his guitar's once soothing melodies. It was as if a part of him had been ripped away, leaving a gaping hole in his heart.

Under the relentless glare of the sun, Bo managed to rise to his feet, his legs shaky but defiant. His surroundings were unfamiliar, an expanse of barren wasteland stretching as far as his eyes could see, dotted with sparse vegetation and rocky outcrops. The once familiar sounds of his clan, the bustling life of Ashenrock Hollow, were replaced by the lonely hum of the wind.

With no clear direction or purpose, he began to walk. His movements were robotic, each step a monumental effort. His mind was a whirlwind of thoughts, questions with no answers, regrets and fears tangling into a dark knot. But in this moment, the only thing he could do was put one foot in front of the other. To keep moving. To survive.

The sun bore down upon him mercilessly as he trudged through the wasteland. His body screamed in protest, his muscles aching, his throat parched. But Bo continued on, driven by a primal instinct to endure. His journey had just begun.

As Bo made his way through the desolate wasteland, the passage of time seemed to blur into an indistinguishable haze. The sun would rise, casting long, harsh shadows on the rough terrain, and then fall, replaced by a cold, indifferent moon. This cycle repeated itself more times than Bo could count, each day indistinguishable from the last.

His Orcish constitution was formidable, a trait of the resilience of his kind. Their bodies were built for endurance, capable of withstanding the harshest of environments. But even for Bo, the lack of sustenance was beginning to take its toll. His stomach churned with hunger, a hollow ache that gnawed at him relentlessly. The lack of water was even worse. His throat felt as though it was lined with sandpaper, each breath causing a painful scratch.

The relentless sun, the unending expanse of wasteland, the harsh winds, the isolation, all of it combined to form a grim symphony of desolation. It was a daunting reality he had to face.

Yet, in spite of it all, Bo persevered. He walked under the sweltering sun, the wind beating against his skin. His legs moved with mechanical monotony and his body cried out for rest, for sustenance, but Bo pushed onward.

He was not just an Orc; he was a Firetusk. Even in exile, even in the face of adversity, he would not yield. And so, he trudged on, his shattered guitar in tow, a lone figure against the desolate backdrop of the wastelands.

Out here in the heart of the Gorgoroth Flats, Bo felt as lost as a leaf adrift on a raging river. His knowledge of the world was limited to the boundaries of Ashenrock Hollow, the home he had known his whole life. He had never ventured more than an hour's hike away from the confines of his village, from the safety of his tribe. Yet, here he was, cast adrift in an unending expanse of barren land.

His surroundings were alien to him. The jagged rocks, the sparse vegetation, the relentless winds, all were unfamiliar. The landmarks he had grown up with – the towering peaks of Ashenrock, the twisted grove of ironbark trees, the rushing waters of the Thunderous Roar – were nowhere to be seen. In their place was an unforgiving wasteland, bereft of any comfort or familiarity.

Bo had no map, no compass, no guide. He didn't know which way was north or south, east or west. He was disoriented, like a ship lost at sea, with no stars to guide him. But he knew he couldn't just stand there, couldn't just surrender to despair. So, he chose a direction at random and started walking, his broken guitar his only companion.

As the days merged into a seamless, timeless blur, Bo's mind teetered on the brink of desolation. His confidence, once a flaming torch, had now been reduced to mere embers, flickering in the harsh winds of uncertainty. Self-belief, a trait he once wore like a second skin, was now a distant memory, fading into the abyss of his broken spirit.

The wilderness around him was as barren as his psyche,

his lone figure etching a path through the stark Gruul Wastelands. He subsisted on what meagre sustenance he could find, but the acrid leaves of desert flora, the dried berries from thorny bushes, and the sweet sap of the jiruba cactus were a poor substitute for the hearty meals he was once accustomed to.

His once vibrant world was now reduced to a monotonous cycle of finding food, water, and shelter. The absence of any distinct goal, any sense of purpose, was as tormenting as the physical hardship. Bo was reduced to an aimless wanderer, walking not towards something, but away from the ruins of his former self.

In the midst of his endless trek, a peculiar sound pierced the repetitive cycle of his footfalls. It was an anomaly in the barren expanse, an unexpected interruption in the otherwise predictable landscape.

The sound was rhythmic, oddly musical in its own way, clashing with the stark emptiness of the surrounding wilderness. It was a curious distraction that piqued Bo's attention, drawing him out of his stupor. His fatigue-laden eyes darted around the area, hunting for the origin of this incongruous noise that had broken the overwhelming quietude of the wastelands.

As Bo's attention clung to the sound, its nature became clear. It was an animal's cry – frantic, desperate, and filled with fear. Its echoes sliced through the wilderness, and the noise was unmistakably that of a creature in anguish, a call for help resonating with a sense of urgency that Bo couldn't ignore.

Bo's eyes darted around, scanning the environment for the source of the cry. But the arid expanse around him offered no clear signs of life. His eyes squinted, strained by the harsh sunlight and the shimmering heat haze that danced above the parched ground. His vision was blurry, the world around him reduced to a washed-out blur of tan and blue, unhelpful in his quest to locate the distressed creature.

The sound echoed through the air once more, less a cry now than a tired whimper. The weakness in the tone tugged at Bo's heart, stirring something within him. The sun's harsh glare made it hard to focus on the spot from where the sound seemed to originate, but there, amidst the barren expanse of the wasteland, a faint tremble of movement caught his eye. Against the backdrop of endless dust and dirt, this minuscule shift felt like an explosion of activity, drawing him towards it.

Bo lurched forward, driven by a newfound sense of purpose. His heavy feet dug into the loose sand, each step propelling him closer to the source of the whimpering sound. His pace was frenzied, reckless even, and his feet slipped out from under him. With a thud, he hit the sand, tumbled, and rolled, losing control of his movement. Sand sprayed around him as he careened down a shallow incline that had blended in with the backdrop, his body rumbling against the coarse grains until he finally came to a stop at the bottom, breathless and covered in dust.

As Bo raised his head he was met by the large, serious eyes of the creature. They held an intensity that was both unsettling and captivating. The creature seemed to be taking Bo's measure, assessing him as friend or foe. It was canine-like in appearance, its size akin to that of a large wolf, but its features were far more menacing. Its body was lean and muscular, covered in rough, mottled fur that seemed to bristle with a life of its own. Its snout was elongated, filled with an intimidating array of razor-sharp teeth that glistened under the harsh sunlight.

The teeth were clearly meant for ripping and tearing, designed to incapacitate prey with ruthless efficiency. Its eyes were a piercing amber, full of untamed wildness, yet, at this moment, they reflected only pain and fear. Large ears, spiked at the tips, lay flat against its head, a clear sign of distress. Its tail, thick and bush-like, was tucked between its hind legs. Despite its fearsome appearance, the creature was clearly in a state of vulnerability, whimpering pitifully as it lay immobile in the shadow of the shrub. It was unlike anything Bo had seen, brought into the pits but it still looked every bit as intimidating. He had no clue what the creature was, causing him to have a mixture of curious apprehension grip him.

In a surprising display of trust, or perhaps sheer exhaustion, the creature's eyes softened as it regarded Bo. It raised its head and extended its tongue, licking the sand and grime from Bo's cheek. The action was so tender and at odds with the creature's fearsome appearance, it took Bo completely by surprise.

Bo found himself taken aback by the creature's sudden display of tenderness. After the bitter and cruel treatment he had received from his own clan, the last thing he expected was to find kindness in the heart of such a beast. He was familiar with rejection, with hostility, and with the cold indifference of his own people. But this . . . this was different.

As Bo moved his hand to the creature's head, he was met by the rough, almost spiky texture of its fur. It was coarse and dense, a far cry from the softness he might have expected. Each strand felt like a tiny, rigid spine under his fingers, a natural armour against the harshness of the wasteland they both now inhabited.

Running his fingers through the creature's fur, he felt

the sharp prickles tug gently at his skin, a sensation that was at once strange yet somehow comforting. Despite its intimidating appearance and the razor-sharp teeth that filled its maw, the creature exuded an almost endearing vulnerability in its subdued state, its large eyes looking up at Bo with an implicit trust. As he continued to stroke its head, he could feel the creature lean into his touch, its whimpering cries slowly fading into contented, quiet breaths.

"Just what are you?" Bo asked. While gently stroking the creature, Bo's attention was drawn to a subtle whimper, a slightly different tone from the ones before. Following the creature's gaze, he noticed its leg, oddly angled and partially hidden beneath the sand.

With a sense of dread, Bo brushed back the sand, revealing a crude but effective snare tightly wound around the creature's limb. The trap had been concealed under a thin layer of sand, virtually invisible to the unsuspecting passerby.

Bo's heart sank as he took in the sight of the ensnared leg. The wire was wound tightly, biting into the creature's coarse fur and underlying flesh. It was clear that the beast had struggled fiercely against its confines, the surrounding sand disturbed and marked with signs of a desperate struggle.

The snare, presumably set by some hunters, had performed its job all too well. The animal, despite its formidable appearance and sharp teeth, was effectively rendered helpless, trapped by an unseen enemy in this expansive wilderness.

Moving towards the beast's ensnared leg, Bo drew upon his Orcish strength, gripping the wire tightly and yanking it from its entrenched position in the ground. The creature winced, its body tensing with fear and pain.

"Shh, shh, shh," Bo murmured softly, his voice low and soothing as he stroked the creature's head with one hand while keeping a steady hold on the snare with the other. "I've got you, you're okay."

He carefully inspected the snare, his fingers tracing the wire that had dug into the creature's flesh. His heart clenched at the sight, a mixture of anger and pity welling up within him.

Taking a deep breath, he looked into the creature's eyes, his voice steady and reassuring. "Listen to me, friend. You need to stay calm. The more you struggle, the tighter this damned thing is gonna get. I need you to trust me, alright?"

It was as though the beast understood his words. With a resigned whimper, it slowly lowered its body onto the sandy terrain, gingerly extending its trapped leg towards Bo. Its large, trusting eyes remained locked onto Bo's, a silent understanding shimmering within them.

For a moment, Bo was stunned. He had never seen an animal respond to words in such a way. But he shook off his surprise, focusing on the task at hand. The animal had entrusted its wellbeing to him, and he would not let it down.

He gently took hold of the creature's leg, murmuring words of reassurance as he worked on loosening the snare. Every so often, he would glance up at the beast, checking for any signs of discomfort or panic. But the creature remained calm, its gaze never wavering from Bo's, reflecting a degree of trust that Bo hadn't felt in a long time.

With the creature lying placid, Bo slowly began to work on the snare. His strong Orcish fingers eased the tension, carefully manipulating the cruel trap. The snare was stubborn, biting into the creature's leg, but Bo didn't rush. He knew any sudden movement could cause more harm than good.

Finally, after several heart-pounding minutes, the snare slackened. With one final tug, Bo managed to unhook it completely from the creature's leg, freeing it from the trap.

He exhaled a breath he hadn't realised he'd been holding. Looking down at the creature, he saw its leg was bloodied and bruised, but it was free. A wave of relief washed over him. He'd done it. He'd helped this creature in a way that no one in his former clan would have.

A sudden growl echoed through the barren landscape, and before Bo could react, the creature pivoted on its hind legs and launched itself at him. Bo found himself sprawled on his back, the breath knocked out of him as the creature's full weight came crashing down, pinning him to the gritty earth beneath.

Its powerful form completely immobilised him. Bo could only stare up at the creature, whose growl had now quietened to a mere rumble. This was it, Bo thought, this was how his exile would end, not by starvation or dehydration, but by the jaws of the very creature he'd just freed.

Expecting the worst, Bo closed his eyes, his body tensing as he prepared for the agonising grip of the creature's jaws. But instead of pain, a wet sensation spread across his face. He cracked open his eyes, only to see the creature's massive tongue lapping at his face, causing an unexpected ticklish sensation.

A bubble of laughter escaped Bo's lips. "Stop, stop, stop," he protested, shielding his face with his hands. The creature, however, seemed to revel in this newfound playfulness, persisting in its affectionate onslaught. Despite his initial fear, Bo found himself laughing and wrestling with the creature, its terrifying appearance now replaced by an endearing display of gratitude. For the first time since his exile, Bo felt a sense of warmth and companionship. This terrifying creature, a stranger in the wastelands, had shown him more kindness than his own clan ever did.

Picking himself off the ground, Bo dusted the sand off his leathery skin. He looked at the creature, its deadly teeth concealed behind a playfully wagging tail and affectionate eyes. Bo extended a hand, pointing out into the vast wasteland. "You are free," he said, his voice softer than he'd expected.

But instead of running off, the creature tilted its head, its tail wagging even more enthusiastically. It nuzzled its head against Bo's large hand, a gesture that sent a warm surge through Bo's veins. Then, with an air of finality, the beast sat down in front of Bo, its gaze steady and determined. There was no doubt about it: the creature had chosen to stay. Bo found himself chuckling at the absurdity and beauty of the situation. Stranded and exiled, he had made a friend in the loneliest of places.

"You want to stay with me, buddy?" Bo asked, looking down at the animal. Its tail wagged even more vigorously, the spikes on its back quivering with each wag. Bo couldn't help but chuckle, a genuine, warm laugh that echoed through the barren landscape.

"Okay then," he continued, scratching the creature behind its ear, a spot it seemed to particularly enjoy. "If you're going to stick with me, we're going to have to come up with a name for you. I haven't got a clue what you are."

He paused, mulling over potential names. His gaze fell on the broken guitar lying next to him, a painful reminder of his past. But perhaps, he thought, it could also serve as inspiration.

Bo mused aloud, "What about Gruumsh, after the Orcish deity?"

The creature growled, the fur on its back bristling.

"Alright, not a fan of that one. How about Mok'nathal? It means 'sons of the beast' in the old tongue."

The creature turned its head away, almost in a huff.

"No? Okay, okay. Let's see . . . What about Ogrun? It's a good, strong Orcish name."

The creature lifted its leg, placing it over its eyes, as if trying to hide itself from such a suggestion.

"Alright, alright! I get it. You don't want an Orcish name," Bo said, chuckling.

Bo's mind spun with the task of finding a suitable name, his knowledge largely filled with Orcish customs, names, and traditions. He thought of the few interactions he'd had beyond his clan. Most of these interactions were distant memories of merchants passing through Ashenrock Hollow or tales told by wandering bards.

His mind drifted back to the songs and stories shared around the crackling fires, tales of legendary heroes, fearsome monsters, and mythical lands. His thoughts landed on the bards themselves, their names that echoed through the ages, their songs that stirred the soul, their stories that ignited the imagination.

A smile spread across his face as an idea began to take shape. These bards, much like him, had a way of connecting with others through their music. They were wanderers, each one unique yet bound by a common thread: their love for music and storytelling.

Bo's thoughts meandered through the long list of bards he had heard of, or whose songs he had heard. There was the legendary Elven minstrel Elerion Silverstring, who could make the trees sway to his melodies. There was the

Gnome bard Thimbledorf Pwent, whose tales of his home-land brought laughter and tears in equal measure. And of course, the inimitable Dwarven skald, Hrothgar Ironvoice, who could make a mountain quake with his ballads.

But one name resonated more than others, one bard who had the most profound impact on Bo – Bertrand Radcliffe. Bo had heard of Bertrand Radcliffe in hushed whispers and songs that travelled through the plains of Anashtarr, his motherland. Bertrand was not an Orc, but his voice transcended the barriers of race and culture. His music was filled with stories of courage and loss, love and longing, pain and hope.

Bo had once had the pleasure of seeing Bertrand perform live when he had passed through Ashenrock Hollow. It was a memory etched in his heart, one that had stirred a deep longing within him to create music that could touch souls just as Bertrand's did.

Staring into the creature's eyes, Bo said, "How about Radcliffe? After Bertrand Radcliffe, the greatest bard I've ever known."

The creature seemed to ponder the name for a moment before letting out an enthusiastic grunt, tail wagging vigorously.

Bo chuckled, patting the creature's head. "Radcliffe it is then."

5

As Bo and Radcliffe trekked further into the vast expanse of the Gorgoroth Flats, Bo found solace in the silent companionship of the unusual creature. Words were unnecessary between them; their bond was one of shared experience, built in the face of adversity and isolation. Even in the absence of dialogue, Radcliffe's presence offered Bo a sense of reassurance, a soothing balm against the crushing loneliness of his exile.

Much to Bo's surprise, the creature's recovery was swift. Initially, Radcliffe had limped, favouring one side heavily due to the injury from the snare. However, within a short span of time, the limp had receded. Radcliffe moved with an effortless grace that seemed almost otherworldly in the harsh landscape of the Wastes.

Bo watched as the creature navigated the treacherous terrain, admiration welling up within him. The speed of Radcliffe's recovery had been nothing short of astonishing. It was a sign of the creature's resilience, his innate ability to adapt and overcome. It was a trait that Bo recognised and respected, having seen it time and time again within the ranks of his own clan.

With Radcliffe by his side, the endless trek through the Wastes felt less daunting. The companionship, the shared hardship, it provided a comfort that Bo hadn't realised he'd been missing. As they navigated the barren landscape, Bo found himself looking forward to what lay ahead. For the first time since his exile, he dared to hope.

As the sun began to set, painting the sky in brilliant hues of oranges and purples, the harsh reality of survival in the Gorgortoth Flats made itself known once more. Bo's stomach grumbled loudly, the pangs of hunger reverberating through his body. He glanced down at Radcliffe, only to find the creature looking back at him, its eyes wide and expectant.

No sooner had Bo's stomach announced its discontent, Radcliffe's stomach echoed with a similar, yet somehow more forlorn, growl. The creature tilted its head, regarding Bo with an almost human-like expression of shared discomfort. Bo couldn't help but chuckle, despite the gnawing hunger.

"Seems like we're in the same boat, Radcliffe," Bo muttered, patting the creature's head affectionately. The simple act of acknowledging their shared plight seemed to bring a degree of comfort to them both.

Up until now, Bo had survived by subsisting on the sparse vegetation that grew in the Gorgoroth Flats He'd found some solace in the juicy pulp of the jiruba cacti, the spiced milk offering fleeting relief from his relentless thirst. But he was an Orc, his body accustomed to the hearty, meat-rich diet of the Firetusk Clan. The meagre vegetation was barely enough to keep his strength up, the lack of meat and fat in his diet making his body feel hollow. His energy levels were dwindling with each passing day.

Similarly, Radcliffe, a beast seemingly built for hunting, was also surviving on the same vegetation. He'd watch as Radcliffe nibbled on a root or leaf, but it was clear that the creature was not accustomed to such a diet. His lean body was designed to tear into meat, to crack open bones and suck out the marrow.

Bo glanced at Radcliffe and gave a nod of determination. "Alright, Radcliffe," he said, his voice brimming with resolve. "We need meat. And it seems we'll have to hunt for it ourselves." The prospect was daunting, but the need for sustenance was far greater.

Despite the vast expanse of the wasteland and the amount of time they had been walking, Bo and Radcliffe had yet to encounter another living creature. The unyielding terrain seemed devoid of life, offering nothing but an endless sea of sun-scorched sand and sparse shrubbery. For all Bo knew, Radcliffe was the only other animal surviving in this brutal landscape.

Bo scanned the horizon, his heart sinking a little as his eyes met nothing but the same barren landscape that had been their constant companion. The situation was grim, but he was not ready to give up. He had survived so far, and so had Radcliffe.

"Alright, Radcliffe, let's set up camp," Bo said, gesturing towards a large, dead shrub. Its skeletal branches were weathered and gnarled, but it would provide some semblance of shelter. It was far from ideal, but it was the best they had. As the sun dipped below the horizon, casting long, ominous shadows on the sand, Bo and Radcliffe settled down for the night, their stomachs grumbling in unison.

Under the ink-black sky, Bo and Radcliffe huddled around a small, flickering campfire. The flames danced and twirled, casting a warm, orange glow that contrasted starkly with the cool blues of the night. Bo had managed to scrounge up some dried-out shrubbery, and although meagre, it served as suitable fuel for their fire.

Bo watched as the flames consumed the kindling, the light casting long, dancing shadows on his face. The fire crackled and popped, filling the silence of the desert night with its soft, rhythmic sound. The heat radiating from the fire was a welcome reprieve from the chilling night air.

Beside him, Radcliffe lay down, his eyes half-closed, the soft glow of the fire reflecting off his razor-sharp teeth. The creature's steady breathing was a comforting sound amidst the vast emptiness of the desert.

The comforting tranquillity was abruptly broken by the symphony of a gargantuan rumble, emanating from Bo's belly. The noise reverberated through the silent night, echoing off the surrounding rocks. Radcliffe, startled from his half-sleep, perked up, his large eyes blinking in surprise at the sudden disturbance.

Bo sheepishly scratched the back of his head. "Sorry, boy, I didn't mean to wake you," he said, embarrassed.

Radcliffe, however, merely grumbled in response, his eyes squinting at Bo in what seemed like understanding before he lay his head back down, his tail thumping gently against the sand.

Suddenly, Radcliffe sprang to his feet. He stretched out his front legs, arching his back and puffing out his spiked fur. His ears perked up, swivelling as they spun in search of catching the faintest of sounds from the vast, inky expanse before them. His large eyes, glistening in the dim firelight, were wide and alert, scanning the darkness with an intent gaze.

Then, without warning, Radcliffe bolted. His powerful hind legs propelled him forward, leaving a trail of kicked-up sand in his wake. His ears remained upright, like twin banners catching the wind, as he disappeared into the night void. Bo was left alone by the dwindling fire, his brow furrowed with worry as he watched his newfound companion vanish into the unknown.

"Radcliffe, wait!" Bo called out, but his words were swallowed by the darkness. He squinted, trying to catch a glimpse of the creature, but all he could see was the small circle of flickering light granted by his fire. Beyond that was nothing but an abyss of black.

He slumped back against the rough shrubbery, the faint crackle of the fire the only sound breaking the silence.

"Well," he murmured to himself, "it was nice to have company while it lasted."

A nasty knot began to form in Bo's stomach as he resigned himself to solitude once again. The sudden absence of Radcliffe's company filled him with a foreboding sense of loneliness, a feeling he thought he'd left behind with his banishment.

The night sky suddenly seemed too vast, too over-whelming, and he felt very, very small under its star-studded expanse. The crackling fire did little to ward off the chill of isolation seeping into his bones.

A lump formed in Bo's throat. The reality of his situation was threatening to gnaw through the last frayed threads of his resolve, the weight of his loneliness pressing down like a heavy, unshakeable burden. His eyes stung, and he felt a strange warmth spreading over his cheeks. His heart pounded erratically against his chest, threatening to spill over his emotions. On the verge of tears, he swallowed hard, trying to fight back the rising tide of his situation that threatened to consume him.

Abruptly, a sudden squeal pierced the silent night, jolting Bo out of his thoughts. His ears perked up, his heart pounding against his ribcage. The squeal was quickly followed by a blunt thud, as if something heavy had collided with the rough, sandy terrain. Then came the grating sound of dragging, like a heavy object being pulled through the loose gravel. Bo's breath hitched in his throat, his gaze darting around the darkened landscape, trying to discern what had caused the noise.

Suddenly, out of the inky darkness, the spiky outline of Radcliffe's rear came into view. The hound-like creature appeared to be dragging something along the ground. As Radcliffe emerged further into the flickering firelight, the object in tow became visible – it was a large, lifeless creature, its fur matted and body limp.

Bo's eyes nearly popped out of his head as he recognised the lifeless mass being dragged by Radcliffe. The carcass was that of a boar-like creature, its massive size promising a substantial meal for the pair. The boar's coarse fur was caked with sand, but the animal looked surprisingly intact, its body muscular and sturdy even in death.

"Radcliffe," Bo found himself muttering, a tone of disbelief mixed with awe colouring his voice, "you hunted this down for us?" He reached out, patting the canine-like beast, who simply wagged his tail and let out a soft, satisfied huff.

Gratitude flooded Bo's heart as he looked at Radcliffe. The Orc's stomach grumbled in anticipation as his eyes met the hound's. "Thank you," he said.

Yes, tonight they would feast. A meal, a friend, and a fighting chance were more than he'd dared to hope for on this punishing journey, and yet, here they were.

A few hours later, the delicious scent of roasting meat wafted through the quiet night, enveloping Bo and Radcliffe in a comforting blanket of mouthwatering aroma. The boar's flesh, cut into generous chunks, was skewered on a makeshift spit, rotating slowly above the fire.

The heat from the flames licked the boar, searing its exterior to a lovely golden brown. The sizzle and pop as juices dripped onto the hot coals below were like a symphony to Bo's ears, each note a promise of the succulent meal to come. As the meat roasted, its fat slowly rendered, pooling into glistening droplets that hissed and evaporated on contact with the fire, intensifying the tantalising smell that permeated the air.

Nearby, Radcliffe was preoccupied with his own feast. He was gnawing intently on a large bone from the boar's leg, his sharp teeth tearing away the remaining scraps of raw meat with ease. The crunching sound as he broke into the bone was oddly comforting.

Bo, sitting cross-legged by the fire, took in the sight with a mixture of satisfaction and wonder. As he watched the flames dance, the enticing scent of roasting boar in his nostrils and the sound of Radcliffe crunching away happily gave him a warmth that had nothing to do with the fire.

Finally, Bo gingerly grasped the skewer's end, pulling it away from the fire. A thin stream of smoke wafted upwards from the well-cooked meat, causing his stomach to lurch with anticipation. He held the skewer out in front of him, the orange glow of the campfire flickering against the seared meat.

Impatient and ravenous, he tore into the boar, his teeth sinking into the well-done meat. The first bite, hot and flavourful, sent a shock of heat across his palate, the roof of his mouth singed by the meat's temperature.

But the sting of the heat was overshadowed by the explosion of flavours he experienced. The tender meat, seasoned by nothing more than the wilderness it came from and the smoke from the fire, was delicious. It was earthy, slightly gamey, yet satisfyingly rich. It was perhaps a little overcooked, slightly tougher than he would have liked, but that didn't dampen his enjoyment one bit.

His hunger driving him, Bo continued to ravage the piece of boar, his bites becoming less careful and more greedy. The pain in his mouth was insignificant compared to the gratification of the meal, a feast that filled him with contentment after days of scant nourishment. The sight of Radcliffe gnawing contentedly on a bone nearby only heightened his own sense of satisfaction.

When Bo had devoured the last morsel of meat from the skewer, he tossed the stripped bone into the fire, watching as it charred amongst the burning embers. The comforting sensation of a satiated belly began to seep into him, the gnawing emptiness replaced by a gratifying fullness that spread warmth throughout his body.

Leaning back onto his hands, he stretched out his legs in front of him, staring up at the star-lit canvas that adorned the night sky. His senses heightened by the meal, he appreciated the silence of the wasteland, punctuated by the distant whisper of the wind and the crackling of the fire.

Without warning, a burp surged up his throat, a thunderous and resonant sound that echoed across the barren landscape, as if announcing his satiation to the desolate world around him. The abrupt noise startled a few night critters nearby, their quick scurrying against the sands the only indication of their presence.

His head lolled back as he laughed at the minor disturbance he'd caused, his heavy eyelids beginning to droop with the onset of post-meal lethargy. His gaze fell on Radcliffe, still gnawing on his bone, the firelight casting dancing shadows against his spiked coat.

As the mirth from his boisterous burp subsided, Bo's gaze shifted from the dancing flames to the damaged guitar resting behind him. The once-prized instrument was a pitiful sight to behold now. His fingers itched to strum the strings once more, but the neck of the guitar that had once held proud and resonant chords was snapped and sat detached next to the body. The strings that used to vibrate with the slightest touch now hung lifelessly, barely connected to the wounded instrument.

Sensing the shift in Bo's mood, Radcliffe lifted his head, ears pricked and eyes perceptive. He looked from Bo to the guitar, then got up, crossed the sandy expanse, and nudged the guitar with his nose.

His gesture was gentle as he pushed the shattered instrument towards Bo. A soft whine escaped Radcliffe's throat, his large eyes filled with an uncanny understanding. It was as if he was urging Bo to pick up the strings again, to draw out the music that had been silenced.

The creature's intelligence and empathy struck Bo. He glanced at Radcliffe, his lips pulling into a small, hesitant smile. His rough fingers traced the worn edges of his broken guitar, landing on the loose, out-of-tune strings. He gave them a soft strum, the notes echoing oddly in the quiet of the night.

"You like that, Radcliffe?" Bo asked, his deep voice filled with cautious hope. The corners of his mouth twitched upwards as Radcliffe wagged his tail enthusiastically. "Do you want me to play something for you, boy?"

Despite the poor condition of the guitar, the joy in Bo's voice was undeniable. The idea of performing again, even if it was just for a creature he had met a day ago, brought him an unfamiliar warmth. It was a feeling of connection, something Bo had not felt for a long time.

His guitar was in shambles, but Bo was determined to make something out of the chaos. He nestled the ruined instrument in his lap, treating it with the same gentle touch as he had when it was whole. Carefully, he pressed his thick fingers down on the loose strings just before the snapped neck, creating a makeshift tension.

With his free hand, he strummed gently against the taut wires. A quiet melody began to unravel, each note slightly off-tune, yet filled with an undeniable emotion.

Radcliffe seemed to understand the sentiment behind Bo's makeshift music. His bushy tail thumped rhythmically on the ground, sending up tiny clouds of dust each time it made contact. He plopped down in front of Bo, his razor-sharp teeth visible behind a contented grin.

His large, serious eyes never left Bo, watching every movement of his hands, every change in his expression. He seemed entranced, wholly captivated by the sounds that Bo was creating. It was as though he, too, could sense the emotional weight behind each note.

As Bo strummed the guitar, his mind began to fill with words. Clearing his throat, he started to sing, his voice carrying across the open expanse of the wasteland:

. . .

"Walking through the plains so bare,
A lonely Orc, no friends to share.
The sun beats down, the wind does blow,
Yet onward, onward, I must go.
Suddenly from the corners, a cry,
A creature of the desert, about to die.
Rescued it, and made a friend,
And so, begins our tale's bend.
Roaming together, through daylight's end,
Our tummies grumbling, oh what to fend?
Then off to hunt, my brave friend went,
Brought back dinner, oh, heaven-sent.
Now we sit, 'neath the night's gleaming light,
Our bellies full, oh, what a sight!
Friendship found, in a wasteland stark,
Singing songs, beneath the stars so dark.
To the melody, my friend's tail sways,
In appreciation, my heart plays.
An Orc and beast, against all odds,
Walking the plains, against all gods."

The cheerful tune bounced off the sand dunes, carried by the night's breeze. Bo's eyes twinkled in the firelight as he watched Radcliffe,

As the strains of Bo's song began to wind down, Radcliffe's tail slowed its excited wagging. With a yawn that showcased all his teeth, he lay down on the sand, his spiked fur rustling softly in the gentle desert breeze. His head dropped onto his paws and those big, serious eyes slowly closed.

It was a sight that brought a comforting silence in the star-lit wasteland, one that settled over them like a warm blanket. Bo watched as the steady rhythm of Radcliffe's breathing indicated he had fallen asleep, the excitement of the day having taken its toll on the creature.

It was a quiet moment of serenity, and Bo couldn't help but feel a tinge of peace in his heart as he strummed the last few notes of their song, his voice lowering to a soft whisper as he sang them into the night.

"Good night, Radcliffe," Bo said with a smile, stroking the creature's spiky fur one last time. Gently placing the makeshift guitar beside him, he reclined against the rough, grainy sand, his hands cushioning his head.

The myriad of stars scattered across the inky black canvas of the night sky twinkled down at him, each one a silent witness to his solitude that wasn't solitude anymore. But in that moment, fear and loneliness were but distant memories, replaced by a sense of contentment that radiated from within him.

His eyelids grew heavy, a soft sigh escaping his lips as he succumbed to the pull of sleep. Radcliffe's rhythmic breathing served as a comforting lullaby, the peaceful hum of the desert his cradle. For the first time since his exile, Bo didn't feel like an outcast lost in a relentless expanse. Tonight, under the stars, he was merely a bard with his loyal companion, and that was more than enough.

6

In the days that followed, Bo and Radcliffe continued their journey, their bond deepening with each step they took together. Their days passed in a rhythm of walking, resting, foraging, and the occasional improvised tune strummed on the broken guitar. Each night, they would huddle together, seeking warmth and comfort from one another.

One scorching afternoon, after hours of trekking through the arid plains, Bo squinted towards the horizon. There, just where the scorching sun hung in the sky, he noticed a faint outline of structures. He paused, blinking against the brightness to focus. Indeed, his eyes were not deceiving him; there was a town nestled in the distance.

"Look, Radcliffe," Bo said, a new spark lighting up his eyes. "We're not alone anymore. There's a town over there. Maybe we'll find help . . . Maybe we'll even find some new strings for the guitar."

He couldn't help but feel a wave of excitement ripple through him. Here was a chance to find some respite, some normalcy. Here was an opportunity to prove that he was more than an exiled Orc, to show that he had something unique to offer.

A thrill of excitement erupted within Bo, pumping energy into his weary limbs. With a hearty, resonating laugh, he kicked off into a run, his large Orcish feet pounding against the dusty plains. His heart pounded rhythmically in his chest, beating a triumphant song that echoed his rising hopes.

Radcliffe, catching onto Bo's sudden burst of energy, bounded off after him. His strong, powerful strides matched Bo's, kicking up clouds of dust behind them as they made a beeline towards the distant town.

With each passing moment, the distant structures grew clearer, beckoning them closer. The promise of a warm bed, a hearty meal, and the sweet melody of a fully-stringed guitar fuelled their mad dash.

As the town grew closer, its features sharpened in clarity, revealing a unique fusion of old and new. Bo gazed at the town, its aesthetics a curious sight like nothing he had ever seen before.

The town was nestled within a shallow basin, encircled by small hills that rolled gently into the horizon. Buildings constructed from a mix of sun-baked clay bricks and roughly hewn logs lined the main thoroughfare, their quaint, multi-tiered structures reminding Bo of the castles he'd heard tales of in Ashenrock Hollow.

Just as prominent, however, was an influence that Bo was not familiar with. Wooden hitching posts stood outside each building, ready to tether steeds of every variety. Wide, dusty streets were lined with wooden sidewalks, and barrel-roofed storefronts boasted brightly painted signs that swung in the breeze, advertising goods from salted meats to potions and herbs.

Towards the centre of town was a saloon, the lively strumming of a lute trickling from its open doors. Around it, the town buzzed with life. Townsfolk moved about, trading wares, sharing news and laughing, their faces hardened yet friendly, echoing the tough, resilient spirit of the frontier.

It was a sight that filled Bo's heart with hope. The town held the promise of a fresh start, a place where maybe, just maybe, a solitary Orc and his loyal, dog-like companion might find acceptance and a new home.

As Bo crossed the invisible boundary marking the edge of the town, he paused, taking a moment to let the reality of the situation wash over him. The noise of the town, the laughter and lively chatter, the clinking of metal and glass from the nearby smithy and tavern, the faint, tantalising smell of fresh bread from the bakery, all felt like a welcoming embrace.

He looked around, taking in the vibrant town. It was teeming with life. Men and women, children and the elderly, all going about their daily tasks, filled the streets.

There was a refreshing variety of faces, some human, others Elves and Dwarves, a few more exotic races, too – but none with his green hue. Yet, despite his distinctly Orcish features, no one seemed overtly hostile or fearful. They were cautious, yes – he noted the sidelong glances, the children pulled a bit closer by their parents, the hushed whispers. But there was no outright disdain, no immediate rejection. This in itself felt like a small victory.

"Well, Radcliffe," Bo said, "Looks like we might have found ourselves a new home."

Bo ruffled the spikes of his furry companion affectionately. His eyes moved across the dusty, cobblestone street, landing on a wooden sign swinging lazily in the gentle breeze. It was shaped like a frothy mug of ale, denoting a tavern, which in this town seemed to take the form of a saloon.

"Looks like that's our first stop, buddy," Bo said, pointing towards the saloon. His words were met with a wagging tail and an approving growl from Radcliffe. "We need to get you a drink, boy," he continued with a grin, his own throat feeling parched at the idea. Without wasting any more time, Bo and Radcliffe made their way towards the saloon, hoping for a welcoming reception.

As Bo and Radcliffe strolled further into town, they began to draw the curious and somewhat wary glances of the locals. Furtive whispers followed in their wake as the townsfolk looked on in surprise. Clearly, the sight of a towering Orc accompanied by a creature resembling a canine, but certainly not a common dog, was an unexpected spectacle in this quaint, desert-edged settlement.

However, Bo's attention remained fixed on their destination. Upon reaching the tavern, he craned his neck to read the name at the base of the sign, etched into the worn wood: *The Griffin's Spur*.

Unfazed by the murmurings of the townsfolk, Bo guided Radcliffe towards the entrance of the tavern, eager to quench their thirst and perhaps find out more about this town they had stumbled upon.

Just as Bo was about to push open the door of The Griffin's Spur, a voice rich with a southern drawl called out behind him, causing him to stop in his tracks.

"Howdy stranger," the voice rang out, warm but with an edge of curiosity that couldn't be missed. The words hung in the air, slicing through the ambient murmur of the town, causing Bo to turn around. His hand paused on the wooden surface of the saloon door, the mysterious greeting filling the space between him and his aim of quenching his parched throat.

Bo turned on his heels, his eyes scanning the crowd for the source of the voice. Not spotting anyone, a soft cough drew his attention downward. There, standing significantly shorter than the towering Orc, was a Dwarf.

The Dwarf was of a considerable age, evidenced by the abundance of grey and white hair crowning his head. His mane was slicked back, giving him a distinguished appearance. Atop his head sat a wide-brimmed hat, the rugged brown leather hinting at many days spent under the unforgiving sun.

His face was a map of hard-lived years, every wrinkle a tale of a journey, a fight, or a hard day of labour. An impressively twisted moustache curled up at the ends, and his eyes twinkled with suspicion as he scrutinised Bo.

A smile, both wary and welcoming, stretched across his weathered face as he tipped his hat ever so slightly towards the Orc, acknowledging his presence in a silent, yet meaningful, gesture.

"Imagine my surprise," began the Dwarf, his gaze never leaving Bo, "when I heard whispers from the townsfolk about a giant Orc stepping into town." He paused for a moment, taking in Bo's impressive stature and the spiked creature by his side with a discerning eye.

The Dwarf's hand lifted from his side, a simple motion that held Bo's attention as he watched the sun reflect off the shiny sheriff's badge affixed to the Dwarf's chest.

"I keep the peace around here," he continued, lowering his hand back to his side. His voice was calm, but firm, and his eyes met Bo's in a silent challenge. "So, I just wanted to introduce myself and check that there are no ill intentions on your part." His gaze flickered to Radcliffe, who growled in response, but remained seated by Bo's side, watching the interaction with keen interest.

The Dwarf's lips spread into a smile as he extended his hand towards Bo. "Name's Thorkil Barlow," he said. "Pleasure to meet your acquaintance."

As he took in the sight of the diminutive lawman, Bo wore a look of curiosity on his rugged face. Coming from a clan of Orcs that communicated primarily through grunts and threats, such polite civility was alien to him. He observed the Dwarf's actions and demeanour with a mixture of surprise and interest.

"My name's Borag-I, but you can call me Bo," he replied. He pointed down to his dog-like companion who was currently eyeing the Dwarf with suspicion. "This here's Radcliffe."

At the sound of his name, Radcliffe let out a low rumble that vibrated through the air between them. It wasn't a threatening sound, more of a cautious one, signalling his distrust of the stranger. His piercing eyes never left the sheriff, maintaining a steady, watchful gaze.

Thorkil gave them another appreciative nod, his eyes flicking between Bo and Radcliffe as he gauged them further. "Well, as long as you both keep out of trouble, there shouldn't be any issues with you passing through," he said, his tone firm yet not unkind.

He rested a hand on his belt, where Bo could see a badge of office affixed to a loop. His other hand gestured towards the town expansively. "How long can we expect you to be visiting?" he asked.

Bo shrugged. "We have only just got here. I just want to get some water for Radcliffe," he said, his gaze wandering towards the saloon's entrance once more. "It has been a long walk in the wastelands."

Thorkil nodded. "That's not a problem at all," he assured the Orc, pulling his hat lower to shade his eyes. "Just tell Cyra inside that I sent you in and she'll give you both a drink."

His eyes flickered to Radcliffe momentarily, before returning to Bo. His voice dropped slightly, bearing the weight of an unspoken warning, "Try to keep out of trouble though," he said. "Not everybody can be as welcoming to your kind around here."

Bo felt a wave of surprise wash over him, taken aback by the unexpected kindness shown by Thorkil. He had prepared himself for hostility and suspicion, but instead was met with courtesy and respect.

Bo smiled. "Thank you, Thorkil," he said. He clasped his hands together in a show of sincerity, his gaze unyielding. "I can assure you, you won't get any trouble from me or Radcliffe. We're just passing through."

Thorkil nodded, the seasoned creases in his face softening in the faint evening light. "Very well, I trust your words, Bo. Radcliffe. Welcome to Shalebridge, enjoy your stay."

As Thorkil walked away, he left Bo and Radcliffe standing there, the sun casting long shadows around them.

Bo glanced down at Radcliffe. "He seems nice," he remarked.

The beast gave a gentle rumble.

"Come on, let's go inside."

As Bo pushed open the swinging doors of The Griffin's Spur, the scent of aged ale, smoky tobacco, and robust laughter filled the air. A cacophony of voices melded together in lively chatter, creating a hum of activity that vibrated through the wooden planks beneath his feet.

The room was a marvel of wooden architecture; Bo had

never seen a building made of so much wood, as trees were few and far between in Ashenrock Hollow. Here, though, exposed wooden beams crossed the ceiling from which ornate lanterns dangled, their warm glow casting an inviting ambience throughout the establishment and creating an aesthetic charm that felt both foreign and homey to Bo at the same time. At the far end of the room, a long, polished bar counter commanded attention. Behind it, an array of bottles stood on display, their contents shimmering in the soft lighting. A barkeep – a burly man with a patchy beard – was busily pouring drinks, his deft movements, evidence to his experience. To the right if him a woman tended to the shelves, her back turned meaning Bo couldn't make out any distinguishable features.

The patrons were as varied as the selection of spirits behind the bar. Weathered faces told stories of hardened wastelandsmen, their eyes sharp and alert. A group of miners, their faces smeared with dirt and sweat, sat hunched over a table, engrossed in a card game. Barmaids flitted around, their dresses swishing as they served drinks and shared hearty laughs with the customers.

Yet, as Bo stepped over the threshold, the hum of the room fell away. Conversations trailed off, cards dropped onto tables, mugs paused halfway to lips. A collective silence filled the room as all eyes turned to him – a towering Orc and his unusual companion. For a moment, all the saloon patrons could do was stare, their expressions a mix of surprise, curiosity and suspicion.

The heavy silence did little to quell the nerves building up inside Bo. In Ashenrock Hollow, Bo's stature was nothing out of the ordinary. But he towered above the patrons of the saloon, and this level of attention made him uncomfortable, in an attempt to cut through the tension, he lifted a large hand and offered the room a bashful wave, paired with a toothy smile.

He then shuffled towards the bar, the heavy thuds of his boot-clad feet resonating through the now eerily quiet room. Each footfall echoed in the silence, amplifying his unease. He could feel the weight of the numerous stares upon his back, boring into him as if they were trying to decipher the intentions of this unexpected visitor.

Despite the discomfort, he kept his chin up, his posture steady. After all, he had done nothing to warrant the suspicion, and he had every intention to keep it that way. He took solace in the fact that he was not entirely alone. Radcliffe, though silent, was a comforting presence by his side.

Upon reaching the bar, Bo leaned on its polished wooden surface, taking a moment to look at the barkeep. She was a woman of average height with a stern face. Her fiery red hair was tied in a loose braid that rested over her shoulder, and her green eyes studied him curiously.

"You Cyra?" Bo asked, his deep voice cutting through the stillness of the room. "Thorkil told me to ask for you." His eyes held her gaze steadily, hoping to convey his good-will and sincerity.

With a nod of acknowledgement, she returned his gaze unflinchingly, her fingers instinctively wiping the inside of a glass mug with a clean cloth. Her voice was softer than her hardened appearance suggested, layered with a comforting southern lilt that suggested warmth and hospitality.

"I certainly am, what can I do you for?" she replied, setting the mug down and placing both hands on the counter in front of her.

With a polite nod towards Radcliffe, Bo cleared his

throat and said, "Thorkil said you would be able to give my companion here, Radcliffe, some water." His voice echoed slightly in the still-quiet saloon, and he felt a tinge of hesitancy creep in as he considered his own thirst. As much as he longed for a drink, he didn't want to overstep or presume on the generosity already shown.

Cyra gave Radcliffe an appreciative once-over, her smile widening. "Well, ain't you just the cat's meow," she cooed, stepping around the counter to kneel down and ruffle his spiked fur. Radcliffe responded with a playful wag of his tail, clearly appreciating the attention, before lavishing her face with a flurry of enthusiastic licks.

Amidst Cyra's giggles, Bo couldn't help but smile. "I think he likes you," he chimed in, feeling a sense of relief at the friendly reception.

As Cyra continued to pet Radcliffe, the hushed whispers and the stifled murmurings around the room gradually resumed their previous intensity. The clinking of glasses, the shuffle of playing cards, and the rumble of conversation filled the air once more. The tense atmosphere that had momentarily enveloped the room seemed to dissipate, and Bo could feel himself breathe easier.

Cyra, after sharing a last giggle with Radcliffe, retrieved a large bowl from behind the counter and filled it to the brim with water from a nearby jug. She placed it on the ground for Radcliffe, who instantly dipped his head down to lap up the cool, refreshing liquid. As he drank, Cyra gently stroked his head, eliciting another pleased wag from his tail.

Looking up at Bo, Cyra's smile remained warm as she brushed back a loose strand of her hair. "And what about you, hon?" she asked in her soothing, southern lilt. "Anything you fancy? It's on the house, as promised by Thorkil."

"Thank you so much, just a water will be fine," Bo responded.

"Are you sure I can't fix you up with anything any stronger?" Cyra asked, her eyes scanning Bo's unkempt appearance. Even for an Orc, he looked pretty rough around the edges. "You look like you could do with a stiff drink."

Bo truly appreciated the offer. However, having spent a considerable amount of time surviving off the sparse and bland hydration of cactus milk, the thought of a refreshing and clean drink of water was more appealing than any hard drink could be. "Honestly, just a water will be great."

"Sure thing, honey," Cyra agreed, reaching behind the counter to retrieve a clean glass. With a deft hand, she poured a generous amount of clear, cool water from a jug into the glass and slid it across the counter towards Bo.

With a nod of thanks, Bo picked up the glass and brought it to his lips. The coldness of the glass against his hand felt refreshing even before the water touched his lips. As soon as he tipped the glass, the cool liquid flowed into his parched mouth, immediately quenching the desperate thirst that had been lingering for days. The water was pure and tasted like heaven, making his taste buds dance in delight. It swept over his tongue, moistened his dry throat, and brought an almost immediate sense of relief and satisfaction.

He gulped down the water greedily, feeling its coolness spread down his throat and into his belly. It was as if he could feel every cell in his body responding with relief, soaking up the much-needed hydration. The sensation was both simple and luxurious, a pleasure that he had been missing for a while in the unforgiving desert. After a few moments, Bo set the empty glass down on the counter with a satisfied sigh. His eyes met Cyra's, and he nodded in gratitude.

"Thank you," he said, "that was exactly what I needed." All the while, Radcliffe continued his prolonged drink from the bowl, his tongue lapping against the water frantically.

"Easy, honey," Cyra replied with a soft chuckle, her eyes sparkling with amusement. "There's plenty more where that came from." She reached for the jug again, refilling Bo's glass to the brim.

Bo paused for a second, water dripping from his mouth and running down his chin. He raised a massive, green arm to wipe it away, leaving a moist trail in its wake. His dark eyes sparkled as he flashed Cyra an appreciative grin. The cold, refreshing water had a revitalising effect, washing away the grit of the long journey. This simple act, something he'd taken for granted in the past, now felt like an immense luxury.

"Aren't you just a curious thing," Cyra remarked, her eyes dancing with friendly curiosity. As she busied herself behind the bar, dusting off bottles and restocking glasses, she turned her attention back to Bo. "Care to tell me how you came to wind up in Shalebridge?"

7

As the hours trickled by, Bo found himself telling Cyra his tale. From his life as a nomadic Orc, his departure from his tribe, the endless days of wandering through the scorching desert, to his fortunate meeting with Radcliffe. He shared about the close calls they'd had, and their recent feast of the wild boar.

Cyra listened attentively, her eyes widening at the more perilous parts of Bo's journey and laughing at the more amusing anecdotes. There was something comforting about her presence, and Bo found himself sharing more than he ever had before.

The crowd in the saloon carried on with their games and chatter, the atmosphere light and boisterous as the night wore on. Cyra refilled his glass with water from time to time, and occasionally tossed Radcliffe a scrap of meat that had the beast purring happily.

As Bo finished his tale, a deep sense of exhaustion washed over him. He hadn't realised how tired he was until he stopped talking. But he felt lighter somehow, as if sharing his story had lifted a weight off his shoulders. As he looked around the saloon, the gentle hubbub of activity, and the crackling fire in the hearth, Bo felt for the first time in a while that he might have found a place where he and Radcliffe could rest, even if just for a bit. As the chapter of their journey closed, another was just beginning. And with that thought, Bo allowed himself to lean back, finish his glass of water, and feel a rare moment of peace.

Cyra tilted her head slightly, a sympathetic look in her eyes. "Well, it sounds like you've had one heck of a ride lately, poor thing," she said softly, resting her hand gently on Bo's for a moment. "You must be exhausted."

Bo let out a weary sigh, the weight of his journey evident on his features. His eyes were heavy with fatigue, his shoulders slumped from carrying the burdens of his recent experiences. Despite a good meal and decent rest the previous night, the lack of a proper bed for weeks since his exile had taken its toll on his body and spirit.

He looked down at Radcliffe, who had finished drinking and was now lounging by his feet. With a tender smile, he reached down to gently rub Radcliffe's head, the canine's eyes closing contentedly at the touch.

"I've never felt tiredness like this," he admitted, his voice carrying a hint of vulnerability. His gaze returned to Cyra. "But I'll be okay . . . As long as I have this guy with me," he added, his hand still gently stroking Radcliffe's furry head.

Cyra eyed Bo with a sympathetic smile, her hands ceasing their motions behind the counter for a moment. "I tell you what," she said, "the inn is pretty quiet this time of year. Why don't you rest up in one of the empty rooms for a few days? At least until you're a bit more recovered."

Her words were like a soothing balm on Bo's weary

soul, a touch of kindness that went far beyond the simple gesture of offering a bed.

Bo shook his head gently, a humbled smile on his face. His Orcish upbringing had instilled a certain pride within him, a staunchness in the face of charity that he found hard to put aside. "No, I can't accept that," he protested, his voice low but firm. "You've done enough for me already."

He was grateful, but he felt a certain obligation to retain his independence. He was a wanderer, after all, a lone soul navigating the rough terrains of this unforgiving world. He didn't want to be a burden to anyone, even if they were willing to extend their kindness to him.

Cyra's delicate features hardened slightly as she planted her hands on her hips, her voice maintaining its soft southern lilt, yet managing to command authority in the humble saloon. "Bo, I won't accept anything other than a nod of that tired little head of yours."

There was an undeniable sternness in her tone that, despite its gentleness, was just as compelling as any of Bo's Orcish tribe elders. The innate authority of a woman used to running her own establishment and taking care of her patrons was clear.

Surprised by this unexpected firmness, Bo found himself subconsciously obeying. He felt a strange comfort in the strength of her command, much like he had felt under the protective gaze of his tribe's elders. He gave a slow nod of understanding and gratitude, unable to keep the tired smile off his face.

"Well, if you're insisting on giving me a room, I ought to earn my keep," Bo responded.

He knew what it was to work; the Orcish tribe he'd grown up in had always stressed the value of each member contributing to the collective good. Now, in this new and unfamiliar place, Bo found that the very idea of work – of contributing – gave him a sense of belonging, no matter how temporary. It felt right. It felt . . . like home.

"I like your style, Bo," Cyra said, a playful grin spreading across her face as she leaned against the bar counter, crossing her arms. "Now, tell me something . . . Have you ever worked behind a bar in an inn before?"

Bo shook his head.

"Okay then, how about a kitchen? Ever worked in a kitchen before, Bo?"

Bo shook his head once again.

Cyra, looking Bo up and down, took in his muscular Orcish physique. The corners of her mouth curled upward as an idea seemed to strike her. "How 'bout workin' the doors, Bo? We can get all sorts of troublemakers in here come nighttime. Someone of your . . . stature could help keep the peace, prevent my patrons from getting too rowdy after they've had their fill."

Bo, however, immediately recoiled at the suggestion. The idea of playing the role of an enforcer, even if it was to keep the peace, wasn't appealing to him. He had spent most of his life being seen as nothing more than a brute due to his Orcish heritage. And now, he sought to find a different path, away from the stereotype that had been foisted upon him. His thoughts raced as he tried to articulate his reluctance to Cyra.

Cyra's face fell as she observed Bo's discomfort. "Oh, I'm sorry, Bo," she quickly amended. "I didn't mean to suggest something you'd be uncomfortable with. We all have our own stories and paths to tread, I shouldn't have made assumptions."

Bo felt a wave of disappointment sweep over him. His broad shoulders slumped slightly, and the excitement in his eyes dimmed. He was a capable Orc, but his experience was limited. This made him less than ideal for most conventional jobs, and his wish to contribute and earn his keep seemed to be slipping out of his grasp. His heart ached with the longing to prove his worth, but how could he do that in a place so far removed from what he knew?

A brief, unexpected note broke through the quiet murmur of the saloon. It came from Radcliffe, who had managed to nudge his head against the body of Bo's guitar, which was propped up against the stool he sat on. The sound was out of tune and twanged awkwardly. The battered instrument, with its snapped neck and weary strings, had seen better days, yet in its dilapidation, it sang out a solitary note that grabbed everyone's attention.

This sudden dissonance sparked a thought in Bo's mind. He glanced down at his guitar, his trusted companion through thick and thin, then back up at Cyra. An idea began to bloom in his mind, mixing with his nervousness, producing a strange blend of hope and apprehension. His green face betrayed the faintest hint of a smile. The strums of his guitar had always been his own source of solace, a friend that sang back his emotions in harmonious tunes. It seemed so obvious now – he could share his music, his stories, with the patrons of The Griffin's Spur. He could be the bard of the saloon, providing a welcome respite for the tired and weary, a beacon of joy in the midst of their travels. The thought was exhilarating and terrifying all at once, yet it felt so right. He just needed to express this idea to Cyra and see if this unusual proposal would be a solution to his current predicament.

The words caught in Bo's throat, a lump of nerves that he had to swallow down. His gaze dropped to the worn wood of the bar, and he gripped the edge tightly. As he found his voice again, it felt like a whisper, an echo in the back of his mind.

"I . . . I can sing," Bo admitted softly, the words trembling out of his lips. His gaze flicked back up to meet Cyra's, his eyes wide and filled with an uncertain kind of hope. It was the first time he'd ever suggested such a thing, the first time he'd ever considered sharing his music with anyone else.

The confession hung in the air between them, delicate and vulnerable. Bo's heart pounded in his chest as he waited for her response, his grip on the edge of the bar tightening. Would she laugh? Would she dismiss the idea? Or would she understand what he was trying to convey, that he wanted to contribute, to give something of himself to the inn, in exchange for the kindness they were showing him? He couldn't predict her response, but he felt a surge of relief and a hint of pride for having taken the risk, for having voiced his suggestion. He had taken the first step. The rest was up to her.

Cyra opened her mouth, a surprised "Oh" slipping out at his words. She blinked at him, clearly taken aback by the proposal. Bo felt a wave of embarrassment wash over him at her silence, the colour rising in his cheeks.

"I . . . I'm sorry, it was a stupid idea," he stammered, stumbling over his words in his haste to apologise. He rose from his seat, feeling the eyes of the room on him. "Thank you so much for your hospitality, but I must be on my way."

Bo moved to stand, his large figure towering over the bar as he prepared to leave. His face burned with embarrassment, his heart pounding in his chest. He had allowed himself a moment of hope, a moment to think that maybe, just maybe, he could belong here, could find a purpose. And now, it felt like that dream was slipping through his fingers.

He felt a pang of disappointment, but he knew he couldn't impose any longer. He needed to move on.

Cyra quickly held up a hand, an apologetic smile on her face. "Now, now, Bo, no need to be hasty," she said, her words coming out in a rush. She placed her hands on the bar top, leaning forward to hold his attention. "I just wasn't expecting you to offer to sing, that's all. It's not exactly the kind of thing one associates with an Orc."

Her eyes twinkled with curiosity, and she tilted her head, regarding him with interest. "But I reckon that just makes it all the more intriguing. So don't just storm off. You've piqued my interest, and I'm sure I'm not the only one. Why don't you give us a little preview? A wee song, perhaps?" she encouraged, her words gentle and coaxing, trying to ease his embarrassment and persuade him to stay.

Bo's gaze drifted down to his guitar, the broken string stark against the worn-out instrument. He picked it up gingerly, his large fingers tracing the split timber and the frayed strings. "My guitar . . . It's broken."

Cyra followed his gaze. "Oh don't you worry, dear," Cyra said, her smile lighting up her face. "Old Erland, the town carpenter, should be able to fix that up in no time at all."

Before Bo could protest, she disappeared through a swinging door, leaving him alone at the counter. He could hear the sound of objects being moved around, accompanied by a few clatters and bangs.

After a few moments, Cyra reappeared, a triumphant smile on her face and an old lute in her hands. The instrument had the beautiful patina of age, the wood polished to a soft shine by many hands and many years.

"This here used to belong to my grandfather," she said, her fingers tracing over the strings. "I'm sure he wouldn't mind if you borrowed it while your guitar is being repaired."

Upon seeing the lute and hearing Cyra's words, Radcliffe let out a low growl, almost as if he was showing his approval. His tail started to wag as he nudged his head onto Bo's lap, looking up at his Orcish companion with bright, eager eyes.

A broad grin spread across Bo's face, revealing his jagged teeth. He carefully took the lute from Cyra's hands, his large fingers gingerly strumming the strings. "Sure," he replied, his deep voice filled with a rare excitement. "What's the worst that can happen?"

As Bo held the lute, it seemed to be dwarfed by his massive hands. His thick, green fingers carefully plucked at the strings, coaxing a soft, gentle tune from the instrument.

Clearing his throat, Bo began to sing, his voice deep and sonorous, filling the room:

"I'm an Orc with a lute, ain't that a hoot,
Strumming along to an old Dwarven tune.
Raised in a tribe, with no scribes,
And now I'm singing under this desert moon."

The room, which had been murmuring quietly, fell into an awed silence. Every eye was on Bo as his rough yet melodic voice rang out. The patrons, initially taken aback by the sight of an Orc singing, slowly began to sway to the rhythm. Heads bobbed in time to the music, faces lighting up with smiles as they listened to the novelty of Bo's song.

Bo's heart pounded in his chest as he noticed the attention he was getting. For a moment, he faltered, the fear of ridicule creeping in. But he swallowed down his nerves and pressed on:

> *"Songs of the wild, sung by a child,*
> *Of a green skin and heart so attuned.*
> *With every strum, the past undone,*
> *As I, an Orc, play this lute's tune."*

The bar was soon filled with cheers and laughter, claps keeping time with the melody. Bo's voice, strong and filled with emotion, drew the patrons in, creating an atmosphere of camaraderie and unity. It was a sight to behold, an Orc, an outsider, winning over the hearts of the people of The Griffin's Spur through song.

Feeling the warmth of the reception, Bo's confidence began to surge. He stood taller, his fingers strumming the lute with more assurance. The slight tremble in his hands faded away, replaced by a newfound steadiness. His shoulders relaxed, and a genuine smile formed on his lips as he basked in the appreciation radiating from the crowd. His eyes sparkled with a mix of excitement and joy, reflecting the same sentiments mirrored in the faces of the audience.

Taking a deep breath, Bo launched into a new verse, a playful twinkle in his eye:

> *"Met a Dwarf with a hat, gave me a pat,*
> *Said 'Welcome stranger, to our lair.'*
> *Cyra poured me a glass, a lass with a bit of class,*

Now I'm singing without a care."

Laughter filled the room as the patrons clapped along.

With an amused grin, Bo strummed the lute, the room falling silent in anticipation of the next verse. His deep voice filled the room, as he playfully sang:

> *"My guitar fell in a plight, ain't a pretty sight,*
> *Left me feeling quite astute.*
> *Now here I stand, with a lute in hand,*
> *An Orc singing songs on a flute."*

Laughter rippled through the room again, accompanied by hearty applause. As the last note faded away, the room filled with a warmth and cheer that hadn't been there before.

Bo raised his large hand in humble acknowledgement, causing the patrons to erupt in renewed applause. A few tossed their coins in front of him, the glinting currency clattering onto the counter. The air was thick with laughter, applause, and shouts of praise.

"Well ain't that a hoot!" a stout man near the bar whooped, his hand slapping against the wooden counter in rhythm with his laughter. "Best performance this side of the Divide!"

"Play another!" a petite elf with sparkling eyes and a wide grin called from the back of the room, her voice chiming out above the hubbub.

"Who knew Orcs could be so charming!" an elderly Gnome chuckled, shaking his head in disbelief.

Bo could feel his cheeks heating up under the bombardment of compliments. It wasn't often an Orc found himself in the spotlight for such a reason, but he had to admit, he rather liked it. His fingers danced across the lute's strings again, buoyed by the crowd's enthusiasm. The sound of the lute, mixed with the laughter and cheers from the crowd, brought a new life to The Griffin's Spur.

By the time Bo strummed the final note of his last song, the heap of coins on the bar had grown into an impressive mound. His performance had transformed the atmosphere of the saloon. The patrons, usually a mix of hardened miners, weary travellers, and insular locals, were now standing arm in arm, raising their glasses and joining their voices in song.

As he looked out at the patrons, their faces aglow with happiness, Bo felt a sense of accomplishment. He'd brought joy and laughter to these people, a stark contrast to his own life filled with exile and hardship.

His gaze fell on Cyra, who stood behind the bar. Her eyes twinkled with admiration and a radiant smile graced her lips. In that moment, Bo felt a sense of belonging that he hadn't experienced since his days back at the tribe. The world outside, with its harsh landscapes and tougher realities, had been momentarily forgotten. All that mattered was the music, the laughter, and the shared happiness that filled the room. And, for the first time in what seemed like forever, Bo was at the heart of it all.

As Bo's song came to an end, he raised his hand one last time in recognition of his audience. Instantly, a final shower of coins clinked against the wooden floor in front of him, the light glinting off the shiny pieces.

"Thank you," he managed to say, his voice rich with gratitude. His words were met with a final round of hearty applause that echoed through the saloon.

With the music and singing over, the patrons gradually returned to their conversations. The collective laughter and shared stories filled the air once more, the atmosphere now even more jovial due to Bo's unexpected performance. He felt a warmth spread within him, an unfamiliar but not unwelcome feeling. After all, he had, even if only for a little while, become a part of this community. It was a small victory, but one that meant the world to Bo.

Crouching down, Bo gathered the coins that lay strewn about his feet. His large, calloused hands easily cupped a significant portion of the generous earnings. He felt the cool metal pieces press against his skin as he rose to his feet, the clinking and chinking of the coins a pleasant symphony to his ears.

Bo walked up to the bar, a look of uncertainty still etched on his face. As he reached the counter, he let the coins spill out from his grasp, creating a cascading waterfall of shiny metallic pieces that clattered onto the polished wooden surface.

"Will this do for a few days?" he asked, his voice unsure. Despite the success of his performance, he still felt like he needed to prove his worth. He wanted to ensure he was more than just a charity case, he wanted to pay his way.

Cyra, who had been watching the entire scene unfold with a wide smile and twinkling eyes, nodded in response. She seemed amused by Bo's earnestness and replied, "Bo, that'll do just fine. You've earned your keep for at least a week by the look of that coin, for sure."

8

In the quiet town of Shalebridge, nestled amidst the
sprawling desert, an unexpected shift in the
atmosphere was felt, a positive buzz of excitement.
The catalyst for this change was none other than the gentle
giant of an Orc named Bo, and his faithful companion
Radcliffe. Their arrival was met initially with apprehension
but soon gave way to intrigue and appreciation. Unlikely as
it was, Bo had, within a short span of a few weeks, become
the talk of the town.

Every passing day found Bo practicing his tunes, strumming the strings of the lute with his large, capable fingers,
his soulful voice resonating through the rooms of the inn.
Radcliffe, always by his side, would listen attentively,
offering the occasional encouraging growl as Bo refined his
craft. Together, they would pen tales of adventure and
camaraderie, of their life in the desert, and the warmth of
the townsfolk. These tales took the shape of melodic songs
that soon found their way into the hearts of the listeners.

Twice a week, the inn would swell with the townsfolk,
their conversations softly ebbing as the strings of the lute

began to strum. Faces lit up, drinks were clinked, and soon the inn echoed with the chorus of Bo's songs. Even the sternest of faces would break into a grin, tapping their foot to the rhythm of the tune. The music breathed life into the inn, transforming it into a lively hub of joy and camaraderie.

Cyra watched on, a smile permanently etched on her face as she witnessed the once cautious patrons let loose, singing and dancing along to Bo's tunes. She found her gaze drifting towards Bo, who would sit in the corner of the inn, his large frame hunched over the small lute, a tender expression on his face as he sang. His eyes would shine with a certain kind of joy, and it was contagious, spreading across the room like a ripple in water.

The pile of coins in front of Bo grew with each performance, the townsfolk showing their appreciation with their generous donations. It was beyond anything Bo had expected. He had managed to amass enough coins to cover his boarding at the inn for three months, much to Cyra's surprise and delight. With a chuckle, she added meals to his boarding deal, citing that "A performer needs to be well-fed."

Over the course of these weeks, Bo found a place he could call home, even if it was temporary. He had managed to carve out a niche for himself in a world that seemed a stark contrast to the one he had known. Amidst all this, the bond between Bo and Radcliffe only strengthened. The two outsiders, in their unique way, had etched a spot for themselves in the heart of Shalebridge, and they were here to stay. Bo had inadvertently discovered a way to earn his keep, a way that allowed him to share his journey, his story, through the power of song. And in doing so, he found a purpose, a sense of belonging. And that, to Bo, was priceless.

The sun was bright overhead, casting the town of Shalebridge in a warm golden light. Today was a special day, a day Bo had been anticipating eagerly since his arrival in the small desert town. Today was the day that the old woodworker had promised to have his cherished guitar repaired.

The guitar had been kept at the woodworker's shop, a quaint little place filled with the scent of sawdust and old wood. A diligent craftsman, the Erland was a man who prided himself on his work, his gnarled fingers delicately bringing new life into old and broken things. And Bo's guitar, with its broken strings and damaged body, was his current project.

Over the past couple of weeks, Bo had dropped by the shop several times, checking on the progress of the repair. The woodworker had taken his time, carefully examining the instrument, measuring and cutting, painstakingly fixing the wooden body and replacing the old, broken strings. Bo watched him work, his heart full of anticipation and a tinge of anxiety. This guitar held sentimental value for him. It was his link to his past, his comfort in his solitude, and a tool for his newfound talent.

Bo woke up with the sunrise, excitement bubbling in his chest. It was not just about having it back, it was the anticipation of the familiar strings beneath his fingers, the echo of its unique resonance in his ears, and the modifications he had been able to afford thanks to his recent earnings.

After a hearty breakfast prepared by Cyra, Bo laced up his boots, brushed down his well-worn clothes, and whistled for Radcliffe. His trusty companion bounded up to him, tail wagging at the infectious excitement. They set out together under the brightening morning sky, a jubilant pair amid the tranquillity of the waking town.

The woodworker's shop was located towards the edge of Shalebridge, and the journey there was a pleasure in itself. Bo walked briskly, taking in the sight of familiar buildings and friendly faces he had come to know over the past weeks. His steps were lighter, his strides longer. Every now and then, he couldn't help but break into a skipping gait, his heart singing with joy.

The familiar smell of sawdust, wood, and varnish guided him to the shop even before he could see it. Nestled in the midst of weather-worn buildings, the woodworker's shop was a mark of its owner's craft, wood carvings adorning the entrance and peeking out from the windows. Bo's heart pounded as he approached the shop, the anticipation tingling in his fingers. He was about to be reunited with his musical companion, and the thought filled him with an overwhelming sense of happiness. Today was a good day, and it was just getting started.

As Bo pushed open the door to the woodworker's shop, the small, delicate bell above the entryway tinkled merrily, announcing his arrival. His nostrils were immediately greeted by a rich, heady aroma that was undeniably pleasing – the smell of freshly carved wood, a scent as old as time itself, tinged with the earthy smell of sawdust that lay scattered over the shop floor. The scent was intermingled with the faint, sweet whiff of wood polish and an array of different varnishes that gave the entire place a sense of craft and purpose.

Bo's eyes took a moment to adjust to the dim lighting inside the store, his gaze soon taking in the multitude of items scattered about the room. Shelves lining the walls were laden with beautifully crafted pieces, items that showcased the craftsman's extraordinary skill and attention to detail. There were finely carved trinkets, intricate furniture pieces, and all manner of wooden wonders.

Towards the back of the shop, amidst a sea of woodworking tools and discarded wooden shavings, sat the workbench – a chaotic, yet somehow ordered mess of ongoing projects. Tools of various shapes and sizes lay haphazardly strewn about.

Despite the clutter, the shop had a warm and inviting atmosphere, a place where wood was lovingly transformed into objects of beauty and function. It was a testament to the talent of the craftsman, the wizard who breathed life into the inert wood. Bo felt a sense of excitement bubble up within him; he was finally here, and he was about to be reunited with his beloved instrument.

As Bo stepped further into the store, he called out, "Hello, Erland?" His deep, gruff voice echoed slightly in the quiet room, mingling with the soft humming of the woodworker from the back. At his side, Radcliffe seemed equally intrigued by their surroundings. His amber eyes darted around the room, his whiskers twitching inquisitively as he sniffed at the air, catching whiffs of the various wood types, the pungent oils, and the faint, enticing scent of other animal visitors who had passed through the shop. The tip of his tail swished slightly, mirroring Bo's own anticipation.

From the cluttered back room emerged Erland, as haphazard as his shop. A man of small stature and scrawny frame, he looked every bit his ageing years, yet moved with a spryness that belied his apparent frailty. His hair was an untamed riot of white fluff, framing a face deeply lined with the stories of decades past. His eyes, though fogged slightly with age, sparkled with an enduring vitality. He shuffled briskly around the shop, a whirlwind of chaotic activity.

Erland was a symphony of cluttered noise, tools clinking and items shifting as he moved them with practiced ease. He seemed to be searching for something, muttering to himself in a continuous stream of half-formed sentences and mumblings that only he could understand. The sounds of his rummaging created a sort of rhythm against the backdrop of the ticking clock on the wall and the occasional creaking of the floorboards.

Bo watched, amusement sparkling in his eyes, as the old man fumbled about, entirely oblivious to their presence. The energy Erland exuded, his absolute immersion in his craft and work, was infectious. Radcliffe, on the other hand, cocked his head to the side, his large eyes watching Erland curiously.

Suddenly, seemingly out of nowhere, Erland's head popped up, his wide-eyed gaze landing on the Orc and whatever it was that Radcliffe was. There was a brief pause, then his lips pulled back into a broad, toothy grin. "Yesss," he said, drawing out the word in a low, gravelly tone that echoed his earlier mutterings.

A chuckle escaped Bo's lips as he watched Erland, amused by the eccentric display. Adjusting the strap of his satchel, he stepped further into the cluttered shop, Radcliffe padding close by his side.

"Hi, Erland," he greeted, his voice echoing in the quiet shop. He straightened up, his large figure looming in the small space but his demeanour gentle. "It's Bo – Borag-I. I've come to pick up my guitar. You mentioned it would be ready today."

Erland paused in his rambling and tilted his head, his gaze shifting to look at Bo. His eyes, a light blue that was clouded with age, squinted slightly as he took in the Orc's towering figure. He seemed to be processing the information slowly, a faint crease forming between his brows as he studied Bo.

There was a long, stretching moment where Erland was silent, his eyes darting from Bo to Radcliffe and back again. His fingers drummed a quick rhythm against the wood of the counter, the echo of it filling the silence that had fallen. The old man's face was as unreadable as a weathered map, his thoughts hidden behind his thoughtful expression.

Then, his eyes suddenly widened with recognition, a grin spreading across his wrinkled face. "Ah! The Orc with the broken guitar!" he exclaimed, the energy in his voice breaking the quiet tension in the room. His fingers stopped their drumming, instead moving to rummage through a drawer behind the counter. "You must be patient, my friend," he muttered, his voice a soft rasp. "Good craftsmanship takes time, even more so when dealing with a beloved instrument such as yours."

Erland nodded to himself, launching into a lengthy explanation that felt more like a lecture. "You see, your guitar was suffering from wood rot. A nasty business that," he began, his aged hands moving as he spoke, adding animation to his words. "I had to carefully cut away the infected parts to save the instrument. I replaced them with a mix of mahogany and cedarwood, it's a beautiful match, I assure you."

His eyes glimmered with enthusiasm as he went on. "Now, the neck of your guitar was another matter entirely. It was weakened, probably due to the stress of constant tuning and untuning, along with your . . . eh . . . Orcish grip. No offence." He held up a hand in a placating manner, even though Bo hadn't taken any. "To fortify it, I decided to embed strips of mithril alloy along the inner curve. Light-weight, sturdy, and has a nice resonance to it. It should withstand any force you can throw at it."

Drawing in a deep breath, he continued, his words punctuated by the occasional emphatic hand gesture. "Finally, the strings. The old ones were, frankly, subpar. I didn't want to return the instrument to you in such a state, so I replaced them. My nephew, he's a blacksmith, you see, had some galvanised steel wire lying around. I had him twist them into a new set of strings for your guitar. They should last longer, produce a brighter tone, and won't rust."

Erland finally fell silent, his chest rising and falling as he caught his breath. A gleam of satisfaction shone in his eyes as he looked at Bo, clearly proud of the work he had done.

The sparkle in Erland's eyes dimmed, his gaze becoming vacant. His lively features softened into an expression of utter bewilderment. He blinked a few times, as if just awakening from a deep sleep. His head tilted slightly, studying Bo's expectant face as though he were seeing it for the first time.

The silence was palpable, hanging heavy in the musty air of the shop. It was only punctuated by the faint tick-tock of a clock, echoing in the quiet space. Erland's lips moved silently as he struggled to find words.

Finally, he managed to speak. "Can I . . . Can I help you?" he asked, his voice puzzled. It was as if the lengthy explanation about the guitar, the precise detailing of the repair, and Bo's very presence had been erased from his memory in an instant.

Bo's smile remained unwavering as he watched Erland grapple with his fleeting memories. This wasn't new to Bo;

in fact, during his first few encounters with the old wood-worker, Bo had found himself in this very situation several times. Erland's bouts of forgetfulness were as unpredictable as they were frequent.

"Ah, yes," Bo started gently, with a twinkle of humour in his eyes. "You were just telling me about the repairs you have made to my guitar, Erland." His voice was patient, bearing no trace of irritation or impatience. Instead, there was a soothing, calm quality to it, hoping to guide Erland back to the present.

"Ah, yes. Bo, isn't it?" Erland said, shaking his head slightly as if this motion could dredge up the memory from the depths of his mind.

"One moment while I fetch it," he added hastily before turning around and disappearing into the backroom. The sound of loud clattering and banging followed his departure, the din interrupted occasionally by Erland's low, incoherent muttering that seeped through the closed door.

Minutes later, the door creaked open again and Erland returned, cradling Bo's guitar in his hands with a triumphant smile on his face. His fingers traced the curves of the instrument with a gentleness that contrasted starkly with his earlier clumsiness. It was as if the guitar was a cherished possession, and he was its dedicated custodian.

"Here you go," he said, stretching out his arms to pass Bo his guitar.

Bo reached out and carefully took the guitar from Erland's hands, his large green fingers tracing the same contours that the elderly woodworker's hands had moments before. He looked down at the instrument, his eyes wide with astonishment as he studied the repairs and modifications.

Erland had seamlessly integrated the new wood into

the old, the grain running smooth and consistent, the colour just slightly richer where the fresh wood met the original. The new metal neck, dark and unyielding, contrasted beautifully with the warm wood tones, providing not just strength, but a unique aesthetic quality that was pleasing to Bo's eye. And the steel strings, gleaming under the soft lighting of the shop, promised resilience and crisp sounds.

Yet, despite all these alterations, the guitar hadn't lost its original spirit. The essence of the instrument his father had gifted him all those years ago was preserved. His fingers curled around the newly reinforced neck, feeling the familiar weight in his hands, yet there was a newfound sturdiness that gave him comfort. The guitar seemed to vibrate with a kind of potential, as if ready to pour forth music at his slightest touch.

Bo's heart swelled with gratitude as he looked over the instrument. It was more than just a tool for music; it was a piece of his history, a symbol of his journey. And now, thanks to Erland, it was ready to accompany him on the next part of his path.

With his eyes still admiring the handiwork on his cherished instrument, Bo managed to draw his gaze away and looked up at Erland, his expression brimming with sincerity. "Erland," he began, his deep voice vibrating with emotion. "This . . . it's amazing. I can't thank you enough. How much do I owe you?"

Erland's eyes flickered with a wily glint as he leaned back, stroking his chin thoughtfully. "Let me see now . . ." he began, calculating the cost. "Given the work done, the new strings, the reinforcements . . . plus a little for my expertise," he added, a hint of a twinkle in his eyes. "How about thirty gold pieces?"

The sum might have seemed hefty to some, but Bo knew the value of the work done on his beloved guitar. It was more than just an instrument; it was a part of him, carrying the melodies of his life and adventures. To have it restored and even improved was worth every gold piece.

Bo retrieved a small, well-worn coin pouch from the depths of his pack. Its familiar heft provided some comfort, even as he knew he was about to part with its contents. He emptied the pouch onto the counter, revealing a jumble of gold coins.

The clink of coin on wooden counter punctuated the quiet shop, echoed only by Radcliffe's soft whines at the side. Bo could feel the weight of each coin in his hand as he counted, tangible proof of his efforts and the unexpected gift his music had given him.

Once the required thirty coins were laid out, he slid the rest back into the pouch. The pouch felt lighter now, but Bo was not concerned. His performance at the inn that evening promised more coins.

Yes, Bo thought to himself, *this is worth every last coin*.

He handed the coins to Erland, the feeling of relief and anticipation mingling in his chest.

Slipping the strap of his newly repaired guitar over his head, Bo felt a sense of completeness wash over him. The weight of the instrument against his back was familiar and comforting, a reminder of the musical journey that had brought him here, to Shalebridge.

Back at the inn, Bo could feel a surge of energy. There was an atmosphere of anticipation that was almost palpable. News of his performances had spread, attracting patrons from all over the town. As he tuned his guitar, he could feel the room quieten, eyes drawn towards him in expectation.

And then he began to play.

His fingers glided over the guitar strings, drawing forth a melody that seemed to fill the inn with warmth and life. His voice followed, deep and resonant, telling tales of far-off lands, of brave deeds and heart-wrenching loves. The guitar, under his skilled touch, seemed to sing, its voice blending with his own in a harmony that had the crowd spellbound.

Each song was greeted with applause and cheers, coins once again tumbling onto the floor in front of him. But beyond the acclaim and the wealth, what mattered most to Bo was the sheer joy of playing, of sharing his music with others. It was, in his heart, the best performance he had given since arriving in Shalebridge.

And as the last notes of his final song faded away, Bo looked out at the crowd. Their applause filled his ears, their smiles met his gaze, and he felt, more than ever before, that he had found his home.

Afterword

I hope you have enjoyed Bo's tale. As I know a lot of you are eagerly awaiting the release of A War Of Chaos And Fury - Part 1 I wanted to surprise you by giving you a couple of chapters to read.

Please be aware these are raw and unedited. What you read in the final book could differ.

A WAR OF CHAOS AND FURY - PART 1

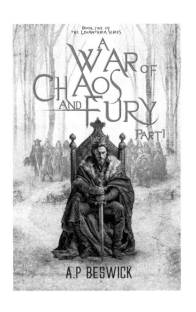

CHAPTER 1 - RHAGOR

I let out a deep, unforgiving sigh of frustration as I stare deeply at the town that sits just ahead of me. It is dawn with haunting, purple haze, sitting deep in the morning sky. If I was a poet I would say it is a beautiful sight to behold, but I am not and I hate everything about this world. When I breathe in the air feels tinged, tainted, corrupted. For others it would taste crisp and refreshing, the morning dew helping to wash away the sins of others, for me it is a reminder of the wretched place I find myself tethered to. Still it is better than being bound to a stone prison for a millennia.

"My lord," Codrin's deep voice, draws me from my thoughts but it does not distract me from my ire. My scouts have been here for most of the last year searching, but so far they have been unsuccessful. They have searched through every brick of the old temple, checking underground passageways. They have not found it." He is wearing black leathers, as he sits atop his grey horse as he pulls up next to me, to take in the view of Thistle. At least that is what they call it now, it had a different name a thousand years ago, but I am certain that it is here. I turn my head to address Codrin, is stony faced, his elven ears, his heritage the only reason that I keep him in my council. That and his desire for power and his usual brutal efficiency when it comes to the people of the land that he governs. He is cruel, angry, torturous, all of the things that I find myself drawn to. It is as though those features have carried through to his appearance, he is after all a hulking mass, broad in the shoulders, his face and skin cracked with scars from battles, some from before I arrived, but most since. One of his ears has a bit missing as if something has taken a bit out of him, a golden plate clipped to the outer edge.

"Then you have failed me." I growl, I take in another deep inhale of breath before exhaling, my anger rising from the pits of my stomach. A rage that I feel from the second that I wake to the moment that I sleep. How I hate being bound by the rules of living in a human body.

"If it is here, then we will find it. My men have been searching, they have been extracting information from elders, I have mages and believers in the old gods trawling through any literature we have. It is only a matter of time." He says, he speaks as though he is convincing himself. "If they fail then, they will have to deal with me." He says with a growl as he draws his hand down to his waist where his fingers wrap around his spiked, coiled whip. It groans under his grip and it brings a smile to my face, he is waiting, he just wants an excuse to use it on somebody, and that is what I admire about him. I say that loosely, he has made this pitiful existence bearable since I was released from stone.

"Are you sure that this is the right place?" He asks.

My eyes widen a Is stare at him and he shrinks into himself, "Do you dare to question a god?" I ask, my voice is cold, like frost. "Do you forget why it is that you still draw breath? It is because I will it, if I find that I am not in need of your assistance you can be assured that your meagre life will be snuffed out like the flame of a candle."

"My lord, I did not mean to offend." Codrin lowers his head, but he is unable to hide the anger in his voice.

"How many people do you think live here?" I ask, changing the subject, my attention falling back on the village. A fence sits around it, about my height drawing all the way around, mapping out the boundaries where it sits. Rows and rows of houses, with thatched roofs line narrow streets.

"The last census has the population just over three thousand." Codrin says with confusion. I am impressed that he has clearly done his own research to know the answer so freely. "They produce good livestock, it is how they have survived so long. Farming villages are able to sustain themselves while still being able to trade. They are in short supply."

"Yet I find them in my way," I say, as I drop down from my horse. "Tell me how many men and women do you have searching right now?"

"Around fifty," he says, still confused by the questions that I ask.

"So there are a little over three thousand souls in this remote farming village, plus those you have tasked with searching and failing me?" I take in another view of the village as it breathes in new life for the day, as light falls on the village I can see the farmers setting about there fields, they have been working hard before first light, tending to there livestock. That is all they are to me, nothing more than a means to an end, and unfortunately they have found themselves standing in my way.

"My mum used to tell my sister an dI stories when we were little," I explain as I draw my sword from my waist and press it to the ground lightly. It is heavy but that Is how I like my blades, I grip the hilt with both hands as I stand before it, my eyes studying the farmers as they set to work. "You see the stories we re told as children of the gods will be far different from the ones you will have been told." I give Codrin a wry look, "That is if you were even told stories as a babe," It wouldn't surprise me if the brute was born through cruelty, I certainly cannot imagine him growing up having loving parents. Maybe he just appeared one day fully formed, as I see him now. I chuckle to myself before continuing. "As children my mother told us about the responsibilities and the burdens that are placed upon them as gods, about the strict rules that they must abide by. Sculpting land, how oceans are formed, how the wind and sun are managed. It is exhausting," I sigh, shaking my head nonchalantly.

"It was exactly what I found weak in my mother and my sister. She created the forest, she was vain enough to influence man to name it after herself. The Forest of Opiya," I say, whilst my right hand in front of me. "See she had all that power, she created a forest where her power, her energy runs deep underneath the very soil it sits on. Yet she still needed man to tell stories about it to feel a sense of purpose. I questioned this, if we were as all powerful as she thought us as we grew, then why was it she behaved in this way? Why was it that some gods only seemed to exist to push back against their own rules, influencing man, giving out curses, tricking people into deals. She couldn't answer. It was something I didn't figure out until I was older, do you know what it was Codrin?" I ask.

He shakes his head, "No my lord."

"It was boredom, what is the use of being all powerful, all seeing if you cannot influence and control the very world that you have created. Just what is the point of it all, bound by rules, even though we were gods that prevented us from walking these lands, from talking directly with people. But where do you think the temples came from? The statues, how do you think people learned to create the se temples, how to worship us. Where the very magic that runs through the blood of elves comes from? We did it, we found ways to bend the rules that bound us and with it life became that little bit more interesting. That's where the curses come from, that is where life itself is drawn, it is all because of us a way of us communicating with the world, a world where we are forbidden o walk freely." I look down at myself, at the body that I now posses. "Rules do not bind me, I found a way to walk the land. Do you think this is the first body that I have possessed? How is it do you think that I was able to instruct this very village to be built. Although over a millennia has passed and yet it is still only grown from a small village of a few hundred to a few thousand. A thousand years is a long time, yet still barely anything exists here. What I search for cannot be found so easily, in fact It is clear to me you are searching in the wrong place. You see the village here sits far higher than the village I helped to build when I first visited here."

I take in another breath and find myself squeezing the hilt of my blade so tightly that my knuckles crack. I pull the blade up from the ground and slam it back down to the earth my power coursing through me and my trusted weapon. As the tip of the sword makes contact with the earth the ground rumbles around us as if an earthquake has hit. Ahead of us cracks in the ground form in the direction of the village and I hear the screams and cries of the people that live there. The confusion, the chaos, it is all so appealing to me. Houses begin to crack and sway as they collapse on themselves as the cries turn to shrieks of horror and screams as people run from their homes like confused ants, unaware what is happening to them. The ground shaking around me centres me, and I find that it surprises the anger that threatens to erupt and I am a picture of calmness as I channel the power of my sword.

"This should make the search easier." I say as I raise my sword once again and slam it back down. The ground shakes even more violently, birds escape the trees where they sit, scattering in the purple sky. The fence surrounding the village topples, showing precisely how useless it was in the first place and livestock make a run fro safety, away from the centre of the earthquake they face. An earthquake that shakes from the centre of their home. The hilt of my sword, glows brightly as I continue to channel my power. In this body I do have my limitations and I can already feel the strain on drawing on it so freely but I will do what I must, I have to find it. It is the only way that my plan will work. I am sure of it. I let out a roar, part in pain, part in anger as wave after wave of pulsating energy ripples through my body as I become a conduit for the sword. A storm whipping up around me until I feel the connection to the power that I carve so badly, the moment I do I twist my sword in the ground as if I am turning a key and a wall of fire pushes out from me. There is a fierceness to it, it is wild and untamed as it immediately scorches the the land I front of me, leaving nothing but shared remotes of what was once there. The heat is incredible and I am amazed that I myself do not burst into flames as I wield my godly power. It evicerates the village in a matter of seconds. What was once there, gone in a moment as if it never existed and in that moment, the screams, the anguish, the pain, they all disappear in an instance. Like a forgotten whisper on the wind, all their pathetic lives gone. What have they contributed in their time on these plains, what have they achieved? Nothing, nothing but a life of misery. In fact if anything I offer them a kindness in releasing them from this world. No longer bound by the rules. I wonder if Quiron will be able to deal with this amount of souls being sent to the afterlife at once. Still it is not my problem to deal with.

I twist my blade once again and the flames draw back towards me until they reach my blade and vanish. I raise my sword in the air before re-sheathing it and shaking my hands. The pain is agonising but I do not wish to show this to Codrin, or anyone else for that matter.

I take in a deep breath of air as I take in what remains in front of me, suddenly it tastes clearer, singed embers hang in the air and a thick blanket of smoke has replaced the morning dew. Some of the stone has survived from the blast but the majority has been turned to ash.

"That's better," I say as I sample the air as I breathe it in, like a cononseur tasting the finest of wines. I let the singe sit on the back of my tongue, before turning and smiling to Codrin. "This should help you with your search, I suggest you start digging."

I turn and hop onto my steed, grabbing hold of the reign s as I balance myself and take in the scintillating view once again. All that life gone, in a moment, but in the charred remnants of this once vibrant farming village is the answer that I am looking for. "Have word sent to me as soon as you find it."

I have never seen Codrin look so wide eyed and shocked as I see him now, sweat beads on his bald head, and it is clear to see that he is shook. Of all the power I have displayed in my time here, of all the time that I have wielded my blade in front of others this has been the most ferocious display of what it is capable of, what I am capable of.

"Imagine the stories that will be told," I quip as I heel my horse and leave Codrin to delve through the ruins. He has to find it, other wise all of this will have been for nothing.

CHAPTER 2 - ZERINA

The winds howl a deafening roar as the force of the sea threatens to rip our ship apart. The fury of the ocean knows no bounds, and she is far from happy. Much like myself. For years we have sailed these waters heading from one bounty to the next, for so long have I endeavoured to keep Esara safe, just as I promised Ulrik all those years ago. Never did I realise when making such a promise that the most difficult thing would be keeping her safe from herself.

As I strap myself to the mast of our ship Esara's revenge as watch through strained eyes as Esara, under the glamour of her magic steer the ship through these rough waters.

Rain lashes against my skin, causing a sharp stinging sensation as water laps up the sides with every wave that we crash into, the boat rumbling as she strains against the powerful force that the ocean brings.

As I watch Esara I swear I see her smiling, him smiling, a dark look in his eyes, that catch the reflection of the moon above. I have often wondered how Esara would look in her own form but it not one she has worn for so long now that I have no clue how she would appear in adulthood. For I have known her for far longer as Ulrik, the now most feared pirate the world has seen. The fear that they project to those who dare to cross them, their anger knowing no limits. Their beard as black as their heart of stone. It is something that saddens me greatly, for they never got to experience a childhood, forced to make decisions no child should, burdened by taking the life of others at such a young age.

My vow is what keeps me going, keeps me from leaving them, after all when a child has experienced what they have, it is no wonder they have grown into such a cold, ruthless adult. It is something that I do not shy away from, after all, I have played my part in their story. It was my visions that took us to Travertine, it was a vision that would steal this very ship and turn to piracy, all with the vow of never letting those who wish to do us harm succeed.

Having failed with Ulrik, who even with my unlocked magic, granted by the elves themselves I was unable to save him. An act in itself which triggered Esara to glamour and take her brothers form and vowed revenge on the King and his fleet that hunted us like dogs. I helped her, I agreed to go into Zorubian territories and I aided her to do just that, and through our actions we brought chaos to the lands of Levanthria. When they succeeded in assassinating the King I thought it would bring all this to an end, that I would be able to greet Esara as themselves once more, but I did not. All I found was someone too young to be burdened with the title of King slayer, someone who stepped into adulthood sooner than they should. Now they are of age and even having achieved what we set out to do, I find their heart only growing darker, their determination to find new treasures long hidden far greater than their need to kill the King.

True our bounties have enabled us to continue to develop our ship, been able to ensure we can continue to recruit men and woman to join us on our foolish treasure hunts. Somehow we are still here, somehow we are alive, if you can call this living.

They insist on me calling them Ulrik, it is as though Esara no longer exists as she continues to channel her magic to maintain her glamour. Aided by the ancient elven waters that we found can reverse the effect of the magic we use, their glamour spell easier to maintain as it uses far lest power than my own flame panic does.

As I continue to watch him staring to keep control of the ship, a wave crashes over them and they let out a roar of laughter. Something is different about Ulrik on this night, he is stony faced but only seems to light up when in the midst of a battle or on this occasion in the eye of a storm created by the gods. I know not what treasure it is that we search for on this occasion and if I am honest I am not entirely sure that Ulrik does either.

The ship groans loudly and creaks as the wood of the hull continues to strain, I fear that it may breach and see us plummet to our deaths, never to be seen again. I wonder if this would be a gift to the world, for I do not no longer know what goodness we bring to it.

"What is it that has you in such a fine mood?" A salty taste in my mouth from the sea air and rain that continues to lash into my face like small daggers.

"We are nearly there," Ulrik says with a growl, he is unmoved, his gaze fixed on the blackened waters that surround us. Waves as big as I have ever seen, rising and falling around us.

"Nearly where Ulrik!" I shout, a rasp in my voice that stings the back of my thought. It is one thing to hold a conversation with someone at a distance it is another to do so when every word you speak threatens to be carried off in the winds that whirl around us.

"You will see Zerina, in time you will see." They say, an almost maniacal look in their eyes, "I know all too well what would happen if I told you."

"That I would stop you? That I would not allow you to put our lives and that of the crewe at risk?" I roar, my frustration rising, faster than the changing tides.

"Exactly," They grin without any sign of remorse for their actions, as though the impact their decisions have on myself and the crewe does not weigh down on them.

I would be lying if I did not say it breaks my heart to see them this way, to see them so angry with the word, hurting in such a way that the only thing they showed to anyone else was cruelty. A far cry from the loving, loyal, fierce, child that I first met when we escaped from Eltera.

"Do you seek to bring us to our deaths, I know you have no regard for the lives of our crewe," I start before they cut me off angrily.

"I do this so that we can do the exact opposite," He snarls, his words wrapped in spikes and barbs. "You will see soon enough, we are exactly where we are meant to be." With this Ulrik let go of the ships wheel, raising his hands away and into the air, his eyes widening in awe.

"What are you doing!" I cry, in utter disbelief at what I see. "Ulrik this is madness,"

"Our lives are in the fates f the gods, if we make it through this, then I will know that they will it, that they want me to find the treasure that I hunt." Ulrik lets out a maddened laugh once again and seeks to keep themselves balanced as their body pulls against the rope that binds him to the column under the ships wheel. "The gods will guide us Zerina,"

The wheel spins so fast that I can no longer see the spokes, only a blurred circle, there is only so much strain that the ship can take and I fear that we are on the edge of our ships limits. The ship shakes and groans louder than the thunderclouds that form above us, the rain becoming even heavier than before, The ship turns quickly one way, then the next, each movement jarring, snapping my head from one way to the other. My heart pounds heavily as my nerves reach a point I have never faced before, not in the ocean anyway. This is it, this is the moment that I have feared for so long, that Ulrik has steered us into uncharted waters that ill see the end of all of us. At least in death I could be reunited with my sisters, I have so many stories to tell them. How I long to hear their voices, to see the smiles on their faces in the afterlife.

"Zerina!" The ship is near breaking!" Darmour's voice reaches me as he fights against the howling winds to peer up from below deck. "We are retaining too much water." He says with a warning tone before looking over at our crazed captain. "Shit!" He curses as he realises that Ukrik has let go of the ships wheel, clown the ship to steer itself, guided by the storm and currents of the ocean. "What madness has over come them," He says.

Darmour is the only other person on this ship that knows Ulrik's true form, the last survivor of our initial crewe that took us to the island of Traventine. He has helped us ever since, he has been loyal in the face of battle. He has been a great first mate, to Ulrik and to myself as I gave my heart to him. He loses his balance and threatens to slide back down the steps to the crews quarters. He slams the hook that is fixed in place where his hand once was and the sharpened tip buries into the ships wood, stopping him from falling.

"Captain, where is it we sail!" He calls from below, garnering Ulrik's attention. "You know I will follow you to the ends of this world, but even I know we need to set course on a chartered destination."

Ulrik looks down and smiles a smile that is more sinister than I care to imagine, the lines on his rain soaked face creasing. "Darmour that is it, don't you see." He beams, "Where we are going is uncharted, unable to be found by the rules of a normal map, by the rules that so often bind us. For where we sail, there is treasure that has not been hidden by man but by the gods."

"I captain," Darmour bellows, his resolve and commitment to Ulrik remaining unwavering, even in these conditions. Unlike myself. His dedication to being the first mate of the ship often leading me to question that if Darmour was tasked with a decision between choosing me or Ulrik that I would not know where he would choose to stand. Not that I would ever put him in a position where he would need to choose, it his resolve, the loyalty that he shows to us both that is what attracts me to him and I watch as rain and sea water pops over him and his tensed arms as he holds on to his position as best as he can.

"Darmour, get below deck," I demand, my worry for him at the forefront of my mind.

"Trust me when I say there is less water up here, than there is below deck!" He grins, "I'll tae my chances here." He hollers into the air in a crazed cheer as if he is enjoying the storm nearly as much as Ulrik is. Is this how pirates think, how they feel. Not to truly feel alive unless battling the forces of the ocean, if so it should be a feeling that I echo, having spent nearly all of my adult life at sea. But it is not, I hate the ocean, I hate these troubled, cursed waters and the foreign lands that they take us. I despise the treasures that we seek, I hate the greed they bring out from men, even though out is what has got us by all of these years. The bounties that they bring have brought us more riches than I could ever imagine, along with the curses that they sometimes bring.

The boat shudders again, jarring me from my thoughts and the ship turns harshly to the right causing me to lose my footing and come crashing to the floor with a thud. Pain errupts in my knees and my right elbow as I slam down with force and slide towards the edge. The ship is turning at such a steep angle that I fear that we are about to roll on our side.

"Zerina!" Darmour calls as I slide towards the edge, only stopping when the rope around my waste pulls against the mast. My torso burns as the rope digs into me, jolting me harshly and I fear that my body will snap in two from the force. I lift off from the deck of the ship and suspend in the air as the ship continues to turn and tip. All I see below me are the darkened waters and for the first time I see the depths of something more black that Ulrik's heart.

CHAPTER 3 - VIREO

"Are you sure this is the place old friend?" Killian stands beside me as we look across the lands that surround Zakron's keep. His greying red hair is almost as thick and matted as the wild full beard that he carries, a beard that I am certain that wildlife could find a home. We stand at the hull of the ship ready to disembark having managed safe passage across the ocean between here and the waters that lead to loch Bragoa.

"That I am certain, our scouts have said that Jordell has been spotted on these shores. We must find him Killian, he is key to our success." My throat is dry and I am in dire need of some water, so I reach for my flask and take a large drink to clench my thirst. It is warm here, warmer than what I am used to, so much though that the air I breathe burns my throat. The land ahead of us seeming dry and filled with baron lands and scorched shrubs.

"Why," Killian asks, letting out a sigh. "Why would anyone choose to exile themselves to this place. It will be a miracle if we don't simply find his weathered bones in these plains." He leads the way and steps across the walkway with confidence. I however struggle with my balance as the height of the ship and the distance to the ground causes my stomach to churn.

Hen I reach the bottom I let out a sigh of relief as my feet hit solid ground, it has not been a long journey, around two days and the crossing itself was relatively calm or so the crewe tell us. However there is a reason why I never joined the Kings fleet, the thought of sailing the seas bringing thoughts fresh from nightmares.

"You ok Vireo?" Killian laughs, "You look a paler shade than you usually do." Slapping me on the back as he makes his way off the jetty.

"I am sure I will be ok," as I take a step forward I swear the land beneath me rocks as though I am still sailing and a wave of internal heat flushes over me. "Then again," I say as I rush to the side and heave onto the calm waters beside us, almost bending in half. Luckily my stomach is relatively empty so it is mainly bile that I bring up, the wrenching noise about as dignified as you could expect. How my life has changed.

Killian laughs again at my expense before setting off once again, when I am done wrenching I fetch another sip of water before catching him up.

What I can only assume used to be a vibrant port is now nothing more than red decrepit wooden, walkways and hollow stone remains of the town that used to be here.

"Do you not found it strange, that no one knows what happened here?" Killian says as he pokes his head into the crumbling remains of a building, eyeing up the stonework.

"It is clear the gods do not favour these lands, I am surprised that they still fall within the boundaries of Levanthria. There is nothing here in these secluded parts." I say as I draw my hood over my head to give me a brief reprieve from the harsh sun above. "The question is, if Jordell is here, what is it that he has been doing all this time."

"That is something I would like to know, too. I don't like being away from the forest, especially when there is a bounty on her heads." Killian cuts a concerned figure as he continues to examine the blackened stone, rubbing his fingers over the surface he turns his hand to reveal soot. "Fire," he grumbles, "What could do this level of damage, do you know of any volcanoes in these parts?"

This is curious indeed, as I trace my own fingers of the surface of the hot stone. Killian is right, the rocks are scorched in a manner that the sun would not cause. "As far as I know there are no volcanoes in these parts brother, perhaps it was something worse."

"What could be worse than a volcano?" Killian asks.

"I don't know, a dragon perhaps." I tease.

Killian gives me a stern stare before bursting into laughter, "As mad as the world is nowadays Vireo, we both know that dragons do not exist, they are nothing but folk tales."

"Stranger things have happened, we live in an age now where gods walk the lands." It has been eight years since the battle of Opiya, when Laith found that blasted sword and unleashed Rhagor on our lands, eight years since that bastard god took control of his body and used it to his own devices. It is why we are here, it why I search for Jordell. If we thought the reign under King Athos Almerion was reckless, Rhagor has proved himself to be a far worse King.

My attention moves towards the deckhand who walks towards us from the ship, he is walking our horses, a set of reigns in each hand. He is a gangly man with barely a scrap of meat to his bones, only wearing baggy pants his skin looks as though it drapes loosely over his bones. His hair is darkened and shaggy as if it has not been washed for months and his skin is coated in a dark oily grime.

"Here you go sirs," he says nervously before passing us the reigns. "It takes either a brave man or a foolish one to wander these parts."

"Thank you," I say pausing for a moment as I do not know the mans name.

"Grimm," he says, "The name is Grimm,"

"An apt name," Killian whispers under his breath to me.

"Thank you Grimm," I say, "please pass on my thanks to your captain, the remainder of the coin will be paid on our return from our task. I pray hope that your captains ship is still here when we return." I would be foolish to give all my coin, especially to pirates. Still it is the only way we could have reached these shores and I am grateful for the safe passage to this point. How the rest of the journey will fare is another question.

Large birds circle above us as if waiting for our demise already, their shadows dancing around us as we both mount our steeds.

"Come Killian, the ruins of Zakron's keep lie south of here, we must make haste."

"Here's hoping he is actually here this time," Killian rolls his eyes at me, an act that does not go unnoticed.

"I must admit, we have been away from the forest for far longer than I would have liked to, but at this stage what option do we have Killian?" I heel my horse into a canter and set off to the baron hills where I have been told Zakrron lies. "Rhagor does not care about our people, he does not rule to let our lands prosper. The world is in even more of a dire state than when King Athos ruled."

"At least no one will dare invade Levanthria as long as he is on the throne," Killian fires back and his tone surprises me. Does he in fact root for this self proclaimed god?

"King Athos Almerion was an egotistical man, driven by the desire for land and power. Rhagor is cruel, he is a monster." It is one thing to believe in the gods and have people on these lands that have been blessed by them, it is another to have one walk the lands so freely."

Killian shakes his head and offers me a short laugh, "Yet you seem intent on going to war with one. Remind me Vireo, is it vanity or valour that drives you?"

A surge of emotion rises up inside of me and in this moment it is anger and grief that burn in my core, the embers of that battle still charring my soul. "It has been eight years my friend, eight years since I watched Laith transform into a monster. I will do what I must to try and save him from the monster that has taken control of his body.

"Do you think his soul can be saved?" Killian asks, it is a question I have faced many a time. "Would he even want saving if he was to know the things he has done since Rhagor possessed him?"

"I can only hope that if we are able to save him that he does not recall, after all it is not he who carries out these unspeakable acts." Letting out a long sigh I look out at the terrain, there is no sign of life. "When Jordell returned from the fae he had with him a staff which he told me was forged from the elder tree, the resting places of one of the are gods. If he has that staff, if it truly does carry magic passed down from the gods then I believe with it we have a weapon that could rival Rhagor and that blasted sword of his."

"Vireo we have been searching for Jordell for so long," Killian hesitates for a moment before continuing. "Do you not think this has become a fools errand? Are we not better served aiding our people in the very camp that you created?"

"Our community has the means and the skills to run sufficiently without me, our path, our mission has become much," I look out over the vast rocky terrain that leads towards a crack in the mountains. "Bigger," I finish as I notice a stone tower protruding from the back of the mountain side. "The keep is here," I smile, "Which means our scouts may be right."

Excitement over comes me and I heel my horse into a gallop as I race towards the mountainside my thoughts racing through my mind even faster. I have not seen my friend for so many years, just the knowledge that he is alive and well would bring me solace. Laith's possession hit Jordell the hardest, how couldn't it, the boy was like a son to him, the two of them travelling the world together. The weather here is harsh and as fast as we ride I feel little breeze to cool my skin as my horse navigates the rocky terrain. By the time we reach a large boulder it is clear that we must continue our journey on foot from this point.

"Come we can leave the horses here," I say, as I wrap the rights around a nearby rock.

"Hopefully they will be here when we return." Killian says, sceptically as he does the same.

I can't help but feel that Killian is growing frustrated with me. "You can always turn back friend if you do not wish to join me, if you want to return to the forest. I am more than happy to make the rest of the journey myself, do not feel like you are tied to this quest."

"What and leave you to have all the fun," Killian grins, "Besides you wouldn't last two minutes on your own. You are too brash, too brazen. Come, the sooner we find the mage the sooner we can return."

I put my hand out in front of Killian and press my hand against his arm top stop him, his frame rivals that of Lek when he was at his most powerful. "Remember he prefers the term wizard, he does not use his magic to cause harm to others."

"I'll worry about what to call him when we find him." Killian says, taking the lead over the rocks.

*****

It is hard to tell how much time passes as the sun seems to set slower here than the forest, it is as though we are in some sort of torturing space as the sun continues to cast down a harsh, dry heat that only serves to make this walk even more arduous than it needs to be. My hands are calloused and sore from climbing but we have kept a steady pace, making it to the top of this pass. I turn to look out over the land we have covered since our ascent and the vast ocean that separates us from the rest of Levanthria. The sight is breathtaking, I do not think I have ever been this high up and I take the moment to appreciate how little everything seems up here.

"Can you believe the lives that have been lost over the years, just for this land. Imagine how much has been lost over the wider world," I say, as my eyes trace the darkened clouds that sit over Levanthria.

"Feeling philosophical are we Vireo?" Killian says slapping me on the back before taking a drink from his flask. His tunic is wet with sweat and he is heavy in his breaths.

"Does it not make you think why it is we do all this? Why we choose to push back against a god, rather than step in line."

"Carfull," Killian says, "You sound a little like the Vireo of old, you have worked hard to redeem yourself, do not fall into the trap of thinking that there is an easier path. People follow you, people trust you to do the right thing, not matter the burden. It is why I still follow you."

Killian is right, although for me redemption is not the right word to suit me. I do not seek redemption. I seek to only repent for the sins that I committed out of selfish greed. It was only when I truly lost everything that I became free, that it opened my eyes to the world.

I turn and continue our trek towards Zakron, maybe when all this is all over I can finally rest.

CHAPTER 4 - ORJAN

"Orjan," Rior calls after me as I stop down the corridor, the sooner I get away from this wretched place the better. "Is it true?"

He reaches me and pulls on my arm to slow me down, his strength has improved over these years but he is still no match for me. As I face him he is a picture of worry, "We must ride to Hora, to truly know for ourselves, but why would our men send word if it was not true." I see panic in Rior's eyes as he takes in the gravity of what I have announced.

"But there are so many who live there, people I know."

"Not anymore," I hiss, "Come we must make haste,"

"And do what Orjan?" Rior tightens his grip on my arm as I make to leave. I understand the boys concern, his anger, his frustration for I feel it too but he should know better than to challenge me in front of others.

"You know I promote, autonomy, that I freely accept questions, but do not challenge me in such an open place. Especially when we are in this vile cesspit." I pull my arm from his grasp and turn to leave, "We ride to Hora, it is here where we will learn the truth."

Rior does not say another word, he falls into silence as he follows me.

"Orjan!" Her voice skips down the hallway and stops me in my tracks, it is like I have been caught in a bear trap. I try to ignore her, but I can't I have things I need to say regardless of the consequences.

Rior stops to but I wave him on, "Go, I will catch you up." I tell him and he continues on his way as I wait for Morgana to catch me up.

"Orjan, wait," she says and for a moment I nearly turn and leave, why am I giving her chance to explain herself to me when time and time again she only serves to prove everyone else right. That she is not a good woman, one that serves only her own needs and not that of others. How else did she end up as King, tethered to false King, parading around as a god in the body of my former squire. Someone I once held so close, I could not be farther away from her having grown close following the battle of Eltera, where we fought of the Wyvern and Barbaraq onslaught together to liberate the people. That was who I thought she truly was, the woman behind the stories that shroud her in darkness.

Her face, it is a picture of concern as she runs after me, hitching her dark dress up as she moves towards me.

"What is it you want?" I say coldly, "It would appear that your husband, or should I say master has been busy taking more innocent lives. And what for."

"You have to believe me when I say I did not know," she protests, her cheeks are reddened and she looks flustered. "I do not know what it is that Rhagor is looking for, why he does the things that he does. I cannot control him, you of all people should understand that."

"Yet you choose to stand by his side, all for the power that you have always desired. Tell me Morgana, what is it like to lay with a god." Vitriol spills from my mouth, I am furious.

Her hand strikes me across the face, in truth I more than likely deserved that for my outburst. It doesn't hurt, my scaled skin is too thick, the blow feels dampened as her open hand connects. My face remains unmoved, as her flustered look turns to one of her own display of anger. "You have no right, you know that it is not like that. Of all the people across Levanthria, I thought you would understand. Orjan we were friends, after Eltera you become part of my trusted envoy. I have told you things that no one else in this world knows about me. Every time you visit for the council meetings, I wait in anticipation of seeing you, with the hope of peaking with you but every time to avoid me as best as you can. Not speaking with me directly or openly like we used to.

"You made your bed," I say, my voice deep and commanding, "your choices are what has defined this moment, the consequences you will have to live with for the rest of your miserable existence."

I hate how I speak to her but I must, to not do so would be a lie for how I feel, her betrayal is what led to all of this. The guilt I feel for Rhagor being here, for him being able to commit these attrocities without any fear of reprisal for his actions, after all who could, he is more powerful than any known being in these lands. And it is my fault, had I not given the location to Morgana, she would not of sent that brute Lek to the Forest Of Opiya, that battle would not have happened, that fucking sword would not have been released back into the world.

I thought I was doing the right thing, now I can see that

my feelings and argument with Laith are what led me to this rationale. If I could go back and stop this from ever happening, I would. Perhaps then Laith would be here as a free man, his own life to live. Instead I find myself at Rhagar's disposal, remaining in the position of ward over Eltera so I can ensure the people's safety. But given the situation in Hora, not even this could be guaranteed. I feel as though I am waiting for Rhagor to snap his fingers and destroy all of Levanthria, everything I hold dear. That I used to hold dear.

"I had no choice Orjan," Morgana protests as she seeks to raise her had to my cheek. I grab her wrist and push it away from you.

"As I said, you must live by the consequences of your choices, as must I."

"I did not know about Hora, you must believe the words that I speak,"

"Why would I believe you now Morgana, after all this time. After everything that has passed between us. Need I remind you of the promise you once made me? "Or was that just a lie to get me to do your bidding?" There is a coldness in my voice, up until now I had thought I had cut off all emotion when it came to Morgana, but that itself was lie for all that rises up from me in this moment is anger. So much hurt so much pain, so many lives lost.

"I have tried Orjan, more than you will ever know." She reaches for my face again and I grab her wrist once more. "This curse, I do not know how to break it. I do not know how to free you."

"Perhaps it is something your husband will know," my reply is harsh like I breathe ice. "I know it is not truly Laith but it is his body that Rhagar controls.

"You know as well as I do, if I asked this of him then he

would know that awe re close, that in itself is not worth the risk."

"As I said, we have both made our choices." I turn my back on her and start to walk down the corridor. "Now I need to go and see how best to support the people of my land to deal with Rhagar's latest display of power. That is if ELtera still remains when I return." I leave her standing behind me, she does not follow and she does not continue her protests, but I hear the heavy breathing as she sobs where she stands. I will not fall for this fiend emotion, I fell for it once and now my heart is coated in stone, it is the only way I can protect myself in this cruel world. To think I once believed that I was falling for the sorceress, against my better judgement, despite the stories that people spread, despite the atrocities I know herself capable of and having done. I will not make that mistake again.

*****

By the time I reach Rio in the courtyard he is waiting already mounted on his steed, holding the reins of my own.

"Took your time," he says sarcastically. I merely growl from the pits of my throat, he knows not to test me, to do so when I am in this mood would be foolish.

I climb on my steed, a large brown mare, standing a good few hands taller than Riot's, given my larger size it is only natural to assume that I need a bigger horse. The courtyard is busy, the ground dry underfoot, guards patrol the outer edge of the walls, making sure there are no breaches in security. Do they think I do not notice their eyes fixed on me, not only a Rashuyan but also with my appearance, they would fire their bows at me without hesitation

129

given their chance. I simply stare back in challenge at the ones foolish enough to keep their gaze fixed on me.

"Come, Riot," I say "I have had enough of this place." And we leave the courtyard making our way through the streets of Askela. "We ride through the night, we have no time to stop and rest."

"I understand he says," He is loyal and has come a long way since I first started training him as my squire. He has become adept with his weapons in his own right although his weakness and affliction is his thirst ladies, and men by all accounts. I wouldn't let him know it but I do not think he is too far off being able to best me in combat.

The streets are in a better condition than they once were, houses are still boarded up as we passed them but there is signs that the city is still in repair. Stone masons are busy getting to work, laying the lower foundations of some of the houses and the markets actually have stalls in, something that I have not seen here for a long time.

To the east I see where the great temple once sat, a sign of this once prosperous city. Before Jareb committed his atrocities, I think of all the men and women that were locked inside and left to starve and it stirs up a fresh wave of frustration. If I had my way this whole wretched kingdom would be dragged to the ground and rebuilt, stone by stone,. It is the only way you can truly forget everything that has happened. In the temples place now stands an egregious white stone statue of Rhagar, his sword pressed to the ground in front of him. As if he protects these people, to my surprise there are a group of people crowded around the statue, leaving offerings as if he will hear them. It is enough to make me snap and I were of course towards them.

"Orjan!" Rior calls after me, but has words fall on deaf

ears.

When I reach them I let my horse run close enough to push them back, before my steed raises up on its hind legs.

"What are you doing?" I ask, exasperated at what I see with my very own eyes, such mindless stupidity.

"Rhagar keeps us safe, we give offerings so that we can prosper." They are like a mindless horde as they continue what they are doing.

"Rhagar is a false god, he serves only himself." I spit on the ground. "You are all fools to believe that he is here to keep you all safe."

Boos and jeers start echoing from the crowd, stones are launched at me, bouncing off my chest.

"Heresy,"

"Fuck off,"

"Lizard scum,"

The words are no worse than what I have become accustomed to but that does not mean I am not disappointed. Word much reach them of the things that Rhagar does, the lives he takes without warning. Why is it they worship him, it must be out of fear. That is the only thing I can think.

"Come Orjan," Riot calls me from my side, "I fear we are drawing unwanted attention on ourselves from the guards."

I circle my horse on the spot and before facing the people who jeer me and throw stones as well as insults. "Know that what has happened in Hora can just as easily happen to you," my words are to no avail, and I look at the large staue once again. The very thing in itself a sign of the vanity that surround Rhagar, he feels he is indestructible. That no one can beat him, but by the gods I swear I will avenge the lost souls of Hora, if it is the last thing that I do.

CHAPTER 5 - YAELOR

In the heart of Osar, I stand amidst the sweltering heat of the forge, hammering away at the steel blade that I've shaping. The rhythmic clang of metal against anvil rings through the air, a testament to the skill I've honed since leaving my life as a barbaraq behind. My long blonde hair, tied into one thick plait, falls far down my back, while the sides of my head are shaved—a bold statement of my strength and independence.

I gave up the life of a barbaraq to live as a free woman in Levanthria, seeking an honest living away from the chaos and violence that once defined me. The loss of my one and only love at the hands of the now king served as a turning point, urging me to change my path and find solace in the fiery embrace of the forge.

As I work, the intense heat of the furnace surrounds me, a welcome reminder of my newfound purpose, the place that brought me solace, the village that helps keep me hidden from the world. With each strike of my hammer, I shape the blade into a symbol of my resilience and determination. Sweat pours down my ash covered face, but I am undeterred, focusing on the task at hand with unwavering resolve.

Through my craft, I have found a sense of belonging in this bustling village. My days are filled with the satisfaction of creating something with my own hands, bringing to life the visions of those who seek my expertise. My work as a blacksmith has earned me the respect and admiration of my fellow citizens, a far cry from the life I left behind, why my people left me tethered to a post, to die alone and in shame.

I am no longer bound by the expectations of my past, I forge ahead, fueled by the love I lost in Laith and the desire to build a better future. In the fires of my forge, I have found not only a livelihood, but a sense of peace and a place to call my own. And with each swing of my hammer, I continue to forge a new path—one that I can be proud of.

I hammer the blade with one final blow, the glowing steel red hot as it is manipulated into shape, I place my hammer beside the anvil and pick up the sword by its hilt and submerge it into the bucket of water besides me. The heat is intense and the water bubbles instantly as the blade cools, finalising the sword's shape. I still need, to sharpen and polish the metal before finishing the detail on the pommel but I am hopeful by the end of this day this weapon will be finished.

"Yaelor," A deep voice beckon's me from my concentration, my thoughts adrift on this day.

Raising my head I see the familiar form of Trivor standing in the entranceway to my smithstore. He has proved to be a good customer in the years since I set up my home here in Osar, his coin helping me pay for this forge, something which I pride myself on building custom from over the last eight years.

"One moment," I reply pulling the sword out from the bucket to cast over it a perfectionists eye before resubmerging it in the bubbling water.

As I step away from the forge and make my way into the front section of my smithy I catch Trivor eying up my wares as he pulls a tree felling axe from the wall and looks over it.

"Such a finely crafted weapon," he smiles, through his thick red beard, his hair is slicked back with oil and his beard seems better tended to than usual. He is a large, thickset muscular man and he checks his reflection in the steel head of the axe before placing it back on the plinth, below the other axes that I have crafted.

"That is not a weapon," I laugh, "That axe is used for felling trees, I am just waiting for Gretia to come and collect it, after she broke her last one."

"It has a sharpened edge does it not," Trivor protests, "Therefor it is a weapon."

"Whatever it is you say," I laugh again. "What is it that brings you to me on this morning. Have you not got farm land to be managing?"

Trivor is a good man, from what I know of him anyway. He does not understand the struggles of everyday life like the rest of us. His parents were given these lands by the King when he ascended the throne after the death of King Athos Almerion for swearing allegiance to him. In the main part his parents have allowed Osar to flourish, with Trivor even stepping in to help the running of the farm lands, which this area is mainly known for. It is what made me want to start smithing here, one when I travelled through I learned that the old smith that inhabited here had passed dot the afterlife having succumbed to an infection which affected his breathing. And two the villagers here made me feel at home, they did not judge me.

My mind can't help but drift to the past I left behind and I am awash with shame for he life I once led as a barbaraq. One filled filled with chaos and bloodshed, one where I did things that I'm not proud of. I can still see the fear in the eyes of those I had crossed, the sound of steel clashing against steel, and the screams of the fallen echoing in my ears. I shudder at the thought of those I hurt, the lives I took, and the suffering I caused.

Now, in the bustling village of Osar, I've managed to find solace and acceptance. The villagers treat me kindly, admiring my skill as a blacksmith and welcoming me as one of their own. But I can't help but wonder, would they still look upon me so kindly if they knew the truth of my past? Would they still trust me to shape the metal that forms the backbone of their lives if they knew the hands that now create had once destroyed?

I wrestle with these thoughts, the guilt and regret weighing heavily on my heart. I've tried to bury my past, to build a new life free from the shadows that once defined me. But there are moments when the memories resurface, threatening to pull me back into the darkness. It's during these times that I fear the villagers will see me for who I once was, rather than the person I've become.

Yet, as I stand before Trivor, sweat beading on my brow after a solid mornings hard work it reminds me of my resolve to change. I've traded the chaos of battle for the steady rhythm of hammer and anvil, and with each piece I forge, I strive to atone for the sins of my past. Perhaps one day, I'll find forgiveness within myself, and the fear of discovery and my past will no longer haunt me.

For now, I focus on my work, pouring my heart and soul into each creation, hoping to craft a better future for myself and the village I now call home. Though my past may be filled with darkness, in the fires of my forge, I find the light that guides me forward, a beacon of hope that drives me to be a better person, one strike at a time.

"I just wanted to stop by and check when the styles will be ready? The crops are almost ready for harvesting and I am sure the workers will appreciate being able to use newly forged, steel styles rather than the blunted ones they are use to." He smiles.

The fact that he puts his families coin into making sure that the farmers have better quality tools is a testament to the drive hand dedication he shows as well as the fact that I know he will be in the fields with the farmers, helping them collect the harvest.

The door bursts open and I am greeted with the panicked face of Orpa, she is one of the children of the wood cutters here in Osar. "Yaelor, Yaelor," She pants, her face red from running, she pants as she attempts to gather her breath. Her light hair clings to her face.

"What is it child?" I ask, but I know what the problem will be before she utters a word.

"She's gotten into a fight," Orpa says hurriedly, "Come quickly,"

The God's will have to hold me back for what I will do when I get my hands on her. A sigh escapes my lips and I shake my head, "Trivor, can I ask you to watch over the smithy for me for a moment."

"Of course," He says, "Anything I can do to help."

"Take me to her," I demand and Orpa sets off back into the street and I follow her at a fast walk. Outside the weather is overcast, the sky darkened by the storm that has since passed, the ground however is sodden and thick mud lines the streets. The streets are relatively quiet with most people sticking to indoors but a man struggles with his cart that he tries to push through the thickened mud. He curses to himself before asking me to lend him a hand but I ignore him, barely noticing his request for help as my blood simmers.

Orpa is further ahead of me but stops at a crossroads in town by the silk weavers and points frantically down the street. "Down here," she says, "she is down here."

Picking up the pace I set off at a steady jog almost slipping as I catch up with Orpa. My frustration rises as I see a group of children tussling in the street and I wonder why no adults have broken the fight up. As I approach a group of four or is it five children writhe around in the mud, ahead of them two more roll around on top of each other. A girl with a thick braided plait straddles another child beneath her a boy, both are soaked in mud, her usual blonde hair barely recognisable. The girl strikes down at the boy over and over, each time knocking away the boys flailing hands as he seeks to strike back against her.

"Stop!" I below, but the girl ignores my words, continuing her assault.

I rush forward and wrap my arm around her, hoisting her up into the air and off the boy, "I said that is enough Gillam!" I roar as I hold her as tight as I can her, arms and legs flailing wildly as she seeks to land another blow to the boy.

"He called me a bastard!" Gillam snarls, she is a wiry one and thanks to the mud she has bathed in I struggle to hold her in place. "He said things about you, might think next time." She spits at him as the boy groans as his friends help him to his feet, a thin stream of blood trickles from his nose.

"Gillam STOP!" I demand, a sternest in my voice that I know will garner her attention, as fierce as she can be she knows how far to push me and she would be ill advised to push any farther. I lose my footing and land on my arse, a sharp pain shooting up my buttocks. I keep hold of Gillam and simply say, "Breathe," stroking my hand over her filthy head. She pants like she has galloped across the mouth of Antar and I shush her gently, cradling her in my arms.

The group of children clamour to their feet and leave, the boy who has had a good hiding from Gillam, has a look of fury on his face as he scowls at Gillam. "Wait until I tell my father about this," He sneers before running off with his friends.

Gillam attempts to break free of my grasp and she nearly succeeds, I hook my arm around her even tighter, "I'll show him!" She says, "five of them couldn't beat me."

"Enough!" I pull myself up keeping tight hold of her, gripping the back of her tunic. "Home, now!" I command as I set off at a brisk walk. Eyes burn into me that peek out from the surrounding houses, no doubt the whole village will be talking about this. Gillam attempts to dig her feet into the ground but as strong as she is, she is still a child and no match for me. I drag her towards the smithy Orpa following closely beside me, casting my gaze across to her I say "Thank you," I am thankful that Gillam has a good friend in her and I appreciate her drawing my attention to Gillam's exploits.

"You shit," Gillam scolds, "Out of all the people to get, why did you have to go running to her.

"I think it is best you go home Orpa, Gillam will not be leaving my sight for some time." I say, gripping Gillam's tunic even tighter as we reach the front door of the smithy. "As for you," I kick the door open and toss her inside, she rolls over the floor and Trivor looks on in shock. "Thank you Trivor, that will be all." I say my eyes unmoving from the stern look I am giving Gillam.

"Of course," he says, exiting quickly, picking the axe he came to collect hurriedly before exciting through the open door behind me.

"By the gods Gillam I swear you are trying to get us exiled from this town." I slam the door shut, nearly ripping it from its hinges.

"Well he shouldn't have insulted me," Gillam says defiantly.

"You need to control that temper of yours, you can't go around thumping everyone who offends you." She is more like her namesake than she knows, her defiance knows no bounds. Was I this difficult for my father?

"The arse called me a bastard, girls can't even be bastards the stupid shit."

"GILLAM!" I roar my temper fraying dangerously thin. "You will hold your tongue or so help me."

She startles and backs down, her body language submissive, her eyes are just like his, full of emotion and fight. "Go to your room, and if you even think about sneaking out I swear to the gods you will polishing swords for the rest of this cycle!"

"But,"

"GO!" I bark, causing her to jump again. I do not like raising my voice to her but she knows how to test my patience.

She gives me a disapproving glare and skulks off towards her room "I am sorry mother," she says and I let out a sigh before heading towards my forge and pulling a sword from the flames. Maybe beating it into shape will help get out my own frustrations.

JOIN ME ON REAM STORIES

Want to continue reading the unedited story?

You can read the unedited version of A War Of Chaos And
Fury on REAM Stories by subscribing to my page. I release
two chapters every week.
As well as this you can also get access to the full library of
my stories in the world of Levanthria.
You can join the Ream Community HERE
Or Visit www.reamstories.com/ap-beswick

PRE-ORDER A WAR OF CHAOS AND FURY- PART 1

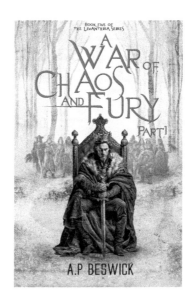

Pre-Order A War Of Chaos And Fury - Part 1

The final story in The Levanthria Series.

Legends Are Not Born, They Are Forged!

Pre-Order From Amazon Here - US

Pre-Order From Amazon Here - UK

THE REST OF THE LEVANTHRIA SERIES

The Levanthria Series

A Forest Of Vanity And Valour

A Sea Of Sorrow And Scorn

A Kingdom Of Courage And Cruelty

A Stone Of Destiny And Despair

A War Of Chaos And Fury - Part 1 - COMING SOON

A War Of Chaos And Fury - Part 2 - COMING SOON

Tales Of Levanthria

A House Of Powder And Plot

A Heart Of Secrets And Shadows

Frost Of Fear And Fortitude

A Frost Of Death And Deceit

A Frost Of Time And Tears - COMING SOON

BUY FROM MY STORE

BUY FROM AMAZON

ND - #0122 - 040324 - C0 - 203/127/9 - PB - 9781916671201 - Gloss Lamination